STORM FROM WITHIN

AN EMILY FALLON NOVEL

MADELINE VAUGHN

Edited by
PANKOW EDITORIAL SERVICE
Illustrated by
BOOK DESIGNS BY SHAE

Storm From Within An Emily Fallon Novel Copyright 2023 by Madeline Vaughn

All rights reserved. Printed in the United States of America. No part of this book maybe used or reproduced in any manner whatsoever without written permission except in the case of brief quotations embodied in critical articles or reviews.

This book is a work of fiction. Names, characters businesses, organizations, places,

events, and incidents either are the product of the author's imagination or are used fictitiously. Any resemblance to actual persons, living or dead, or locales is entirely coincidental.

For information contact: www.madelinevaughnbooks.com

Paperback 5 x8

First Edition 2023

ISBN 979-8-9883268-2-3

Edited by Pankow Editorial Services

Cover by Book Designs by Shae

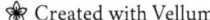 Created with Vellum

To my husband, you are my person, my sounding board, my home. I love you.
To Ashley, thank you for being so incredibly supportive and always cheering me on. Love you.

PROLOGUE

Robert Stanley

Fifteen years ago-2004
Pacing around my desk I start to think to myself, how am I going to come back from this? This is the third mistake I've made and by far the biggest one. I could be dishonorably discharged after this. My naval career will go down in flames. I try to think back to last night, we were all out having some drinks before our pending deployment. The guys from my unit and I met up at a local watering hole around 7:00 p.m. to start our celebration. I remember leaving the first place and ending up at another bar, but from there, it starts to get blurry. Maybe I was four beers in at that point? Not enough to feel even remotely tipsy or drunk. The rest of the night was a blur and before I knew it, I was waking up alone in a random apartment. I didn't know how I got there. Still don't.

I remember the harsh glare of the sunlight as I left one

room and walked out into an open living room. The living room was practically empty except for an old-looking couch and a dark brown coffee table. There wasn't a television, home decor of any kind, or photos in the apartment to tell me whose place I was in.

"Hello? Is anyone here?" I asked to an open room.

My question had an echo to it as if the place had been abandoned. But then why was I there and how did I get there? I reached into my pocket and felt for my keys. They were still inside.

Leaving the apartment, I remember walking down three flights of stairs and out into an alley where my car was parked down a bit. Getting into my car, I started to feel the intense pounding in my head. I don't get it; I didn't have nearly what I was capable of drinking last night. Why did I feel like hammered shit? I pinch my nose trying to summon fragments from my forgotten evening.

Turning the key, the car came to life and my eyes immediately saw the time on the dashboard. 11:07 a.m., Fuck! I missed reporting for deployment this morning. The Navy doesn't think kindly of someone not showing up for sea duty. I looked around outside the car to try and get my bearings. I was not even sure where the hell I was or what part of the city I was in. My phone was sitting on the console. There were several missed calls and a voicemail from my Commanding Officer asking me to report to the station to explain my absence.

The pounding in my head wouldn't stop and I still couldn't remember much from last night. Inching my car out of the alley, I headed North trying to find a gas station so I could ask for directions and, at the very least, find my location. A few stoplights ahead, was a gas station.

I was greeted immediately when I walk in.

"Morning, Sir. Let me know if you need help finding anything."

"Thanks, where is stuff for headaches?"

"Aisle two."

"Thanks."

Grabbing a few packs of ibuprofen and a bottle of water from the cooler next to the checkout, I thought, should be plenty. As I paid for my much-needed items, I asked the clerk, "How far away am I from Norfolk Naval Base?"

"You are about twenty miles away. This is Raleigh Terrace. You good, Sir?"

"I'm fine, I have a headache and it's making it hard to think at the moment," I raised my newfound items to show the clerk.

"Gotcha, well let's get you on your way then."

A few minutes later I was heading back to the station. I knew I needed to stop at one of the base medical facilities to get checked out. It might be the only way I didn't get completely discharged from the Navy. Damn, I didn't know if I should check in with Captain Cohen to let her know I was alive and missed my ship or get checked out first.

Reaching the gate at the station, I drove through and decided to confront this head-on for lack of a better term right now. I'd be upfront about last night and then prepare for a court marshaling or head to the medical facility. The first stop, though, was my office.

Pacing around isn't getting me anywhere, I know I need to talk to her, so I head over to her office. I grab my small voice recorder on my way out. With something like this, I'm not taking any chances. A recording might come in handy if I need to hire an attorney to lessen the blow of the punishment. I look around my office one more time before I head over to make sure I don't need anything else.

Once I'm there, the door is slightly ajar. I knock.

"Come in," a strong female voice responds.

"Captain Cohen, do you have a moment?"

"What the hell are you doing standing in the doorway of my office, Lieutenant Stanley?"

"That's why I'm here, Ma'am."

She removes her reading glasses and has an *I mean business look* on her face.

"I wish I could explain what happened, but I can't. My memory is completely blank about last night's events, but I know that I missed my ship. I'm hoping that confronting this now is some sort of saving grace. You must know it wasn't deliberate, Jack."

"Don't call me that, Lieutenant Stanley. We might go back a long time, but at this station and in this room, I am your superior. You will address me accordingly."

"Yes ma'am. Sorry Ma'am."

"What happened?"

I explain to her the minimal details that I can recall. She stares at me for a moment before speaking, "Have you reached out to the other people in your unit to see if they can provide some insight into your evening, Lieutenant?"

"No, because they are on my ship. My Commanding officer called a few times and left me a voicemail. He is also on my ship and I'm sure it's been noticed that I am not. I wanted to speak with you first."

"Have you been checked out by medical yet?"

"No, you were my first stop."

"We have a situation here that's for sure. You realize you missing your ships movement is grounds for dismissal?"

My hazy night out has cost me my deployment, my

sense of duty, and the trust of those that depend on me. The consequences of last night, are a heavy burden to bear.

"I'm aware, but I'm hoping there is something that can be done. This is an unusual situation. You know I would have been on that ship any other way."

"This is your third offense, Lieutenant; your time here is done. First, you had a failure to adhere to the Navy uniform regulations because you continually were caught not properly maintaining your uniform components."

"I don't know what happened to my items. They kept disappearing. I know that isn't a good reason, but I can't explain what happened to them."

"Your uniforms and the components are your responsibility, Lieutenant. Only person to blame is yourself."

"Don't forget about the unauthorized equipment modification for trying to alter some of the naval equipment without proper approval."

"That was my misunderstanding. I thought you had already cleared it. I took full responsibility for that one."

"As you should have, Lieutenant. I was still in the process of getting authorization when you decided to do the modifications."

Her voice keeps raising as she points out all my indiscretions.

"There must be something you can do. I came here because of our history and because you're my friend, not because you are my superior. I know you have a job to do but I was looking for your guidance. This is me begging you, Jack."

"I said to not call me that. Let me think."

It feels like an eternity passes while she sits behind her big mahogany desk and contemplates my predicament.

"There might be something I can do. First, you need to get cleared by medical and they need to put it in your medical chart that you lost consciousness. That will give you a few days here at the station."

"Then what?"

"I'm getting to that. You will be assigned to the USS Harrison."

"Why the USS Harrison?"

"It's our ship that goes to Ecuador for the Naval exercises with other countries. You will be on a specific assignment each time it's sent out. What I'm about to tell you is not to leave this room. You utter anything about this, I will have you court marshaled so fast your fucking head will spin. Do you hear me?"

"Loud and clear, ma'am."

"There is an organization that I oversee that handles covert operations. A clandestine network designed to facilitate a seamless exchange of classified information. We have a contact in Ecuador that you will meet with each time you are sent out. Your duties will include giving the Mayor of Manta a tour of our ship, overseeing drills between the different Navies and meeting with this contact."

"Why am I meeting with this person?"

"I'm getting to that. You will provide him with the coordinates for our ships and the others that are down there for the week."

"Why would I do that, ma'am?"

She looks at me like I said the most ridiculous thing just now.

"Do you know what's been happening around the ports in Ecuador?"

"I know other countries try to smuggle drugs in and around their ports."

She nods in agreement with my comment. Then begins to speak again, "Providing the classified information to the contact allows him to give that to the Cartel. They will use that to avoid being caught by us or any of the other countries that are protecting the ports."

"I see."

"Is this a problem for you, Robert?"

"Now we're using first names, Jack?"

"Listen to me very carefully. You will navigate this task each time with precision and subtlety. If you can't do this, then we can proceed with your court marshal. You like chess, right?"

"Yes, what does chess have to do with this?"

"Because this is your only move. You've got yourself backed into a corner. But if you agree to this new role, you will be paid after each trip. At some point, you will need to find a few trustworthy people to work with you. I've noticed you and Ted Abbott are pretty close. Maybe read him in but keep him at arm's length. There will be times when you won't be available to meet our contact or one of his men. We don't want to miss that appointment. All of our asses are on the line here."

"Who's been handling this up until now?"

"Nobody. It's been in the works for some time but this week the first meeting happens. You will be representing me when you meet him."

"How do I contact this person?"

She pulls a cell phone from her desk drawer. "This phone has one number in it. The contact. When he messages, you make yourself available and meet him at the location that he will send to you. You have thirty minutes to get to the meet site."

"And if I can't make it in thirty minutes."

"You don't want to find out what happens so don't be late."

"Robert, can you do this?"

"What other options do I have right now, Jack?"

"None, but once this starts, there is only one way out and nobody will know what happened to you. Am I making myself clear?"

"I understand."

"Go see medical and let me know today what they say."

I get up to leave her office, but she gets my attention as I'm about to walk out the door.

"Robert?"

"Yes ma'am?"

"Welcome to EM-Comm."

EMILY

*P*resent Day 2019

"Xander! Get your cute ass down here now or we are going to be late!"

"Ems, we're walking across the street, so unless a tsunami plans to hit, I think we'll be fine."

"Don't try to rationalize this with me. You know how much I hate being late."

Xander comes down the stairs and into the kitchen where I'm not so patiently waiting at the kitchen island. It's still hard to believe everything that happened last year. From Mav and Mel being taken, finding out about our dad and David being killed, and Asher not being who we all thought he was. I mean he was always a douche canoe, but he was a douche canoe wanting to take out our family one Fallon at a time. Because of those events and realizing how short life really is, we have decided to incorporate a weekly family dinner into our schedules. Normally we have them on Sundays, but this week we moved it to Friday. Uncle Paul still owns the house down the street, so we are meeting there this week.

He meets me at the counter and pulls a gift bag from behind his back and hands it to me.

"What's this for?"

"I saw this the other day while I was out. After everything that happened last year with Mel and Maverick, I thought it would be a functional item with a bit of added security."

Raising an eyebrow as I peek inside the bag to see what he bought, I tell him thank you and kiss his cheek.

"You might think I'm being a little overprotective and I know you would be fine, but this gives me a little bit of ease with some of its functions. Plus, it's perfect for running."

Inside the bag is a beautiful smartwatch. The box alone promotes all its functions from monitoring my workouts, sleep patterns and GPS to sending alerts if something were to happen and my heart rate were to spike, it would alert an emergency contact to me and my location.

"Xander Ellis, are you trying to stalk me?"

"No more than I already do, princess. I know you love it."

He smacks my ass as I walk to the counter.

"It wasn't completely selfless, Ems, I bought it for my peace of mind. It works off of Wi-Fi but pairs with satellites. Living on a set of barrier islands, while great, the Wi-Fi is shit."

I shake my head and laugh at his comment expecting nothing less. He hugs me briefly and notices the items I have prepared on the counter.

"Are these the items we are taking?" Xander asks as he grabs the bags already packed with some food and wine.

"Yes, we offered to bring the sides and some wine. This should be plenty for the six of us. I can't wait to get my hands on my niece!"

"Babe, she's a little too young to start teaching her self-defense moves so maybe just snuggle with her today."

My sweet niece was born right after Christmas last year. She has Maverick's eyes and thankfully Mel's hair and nose. That little girl doesn't even realize how lucky she is yet to have such amazing parents and so many people to protect and keep her safe.

"It's never too early for self-defense lessons, however for now I can read to her about them. I'm sure they have baby books on the topic, right? I also found the most adorable baby martial arts Gi for her! It's still a little big, but she will grow into it."

Xander looks at me with his boy next door smile as he walks over to me and rests his hands on my shoulders.

"You, my love, are ridiculous. Maybe save the Gi for next month when Evelyn is at least five months old."

"You're probably right. I'll leave it here."

"You ready yet, Ems, because now we are going to be late."

I playfully smack him on his arm as he grabs the bags, and we head out the door to Uncle Paul's house.

It's a little after 5:00 p.m. in April, the sun has shifted already preparing to set. The temperature is around sixty-five degrees. The house is only a few houses away and the weather is perfect for a walk.

Walking into the driveway as we head up the front stairs, I notice how different the house looks.

"I can't believe how much this house has changed in the past few months, Xander. You and Maverick have done an amazing job with the renovations and helping Uncle Paul."

"He's been a tremendous help, Emily," Uncle Paul says while standing in the open doorway.

Once inside, the front room to the left is where we originally sat on folding chairs to devise our plan to get to

Asher last year. Now it's a formal dining room with a gorgeous chandelier hanging over an oversized farm table. The plywood that was over the windows is long gone and replaced with one-touch blinds that are currently open to allow the remaining light for the day into this room.

"Do you know what time Maverick and Mel will be here? He didn't answer my call earlier."

Xander takes the items we brought into the recently updated kitchen.

"He called me earlier and mentioned that they would be running late. Baby Evelyn has her four-month checkup appointment today and they are heading here after that," Uncle Paul fills us in.

Xander walks back into the formal dining area with a freshly poured glass of wine.

"I know you've had a long week at work, I thought you might want this now," he says, as he hands me a wine glass.

I kiss him briefly and take the wine graciously while I head into the kitchen to put the sides we brought in one of the two ovens to keep them warm until it's time to eat.

We make small talk over the next hour or so until we hear a car pull into the drive. Setting down my glass, I head toward the door to see if Maverick and Mel need any help.

Maverick pops the trunk and I notice a few overnight bags.

"Need any help?" I ask as I head down the stairs toward the car.

I reach Mel first and hug her while trying to catch a peek at my sleeping angel of a niece in the backseat.

"Would you grab Evelyn? Thanks, Emme."

We all walk back to the house, me with the most important item, my niece in her baby carrier.

Mel heads into the kitchen to add the dessert they

brought to the counter and puts some ice cream in the freezer.

Maverick takes their overnight bags into one of the recently finished spare bedrooms already fitted with a crib for when Evelyn visits.

"I didn't realize you all were staying here this weekend," I say to Maverick as he walks back into the kitchen.

"That's why we asked about moving the family dinner to tonight. We want to show Evelyn the ocean and a few of mom and dad's favorite places. Seeing how Evelyn is mom's namesake, we figured four months was the perfect time to start."

"I think that's a wonderful idea!" says Uncle Paul as he grabs the roast from the oven.

I grab our sides of homemade mashed potatoes and roasted brussel sprouts from the lower oven adding them to the counter.

Once everything is out, we prepare our plates and head into the dining room.

"I hate to be all business tonight, but there's another reason I needed to move this dinner up," says Maverick in an almost too serious tone.

I look around the table and it appears nobody else knows what he is talking about, so we all look toward him to continue.

"The trigger that Xander had me install into our system at the Naval base flagged some information yesterday. Abbott is heading back to Norfolk this weekend; he's been gone at sea for most of this past year. We need to watch him and see what he knows or who he's working with now. With Asher and the muscle out of the picture, I assume he has some new recruits working for him to do his bidding."

"Any thoughts on who that might be, Maverick?" asks Uncle Paul.

"Nobody stands out at the station but I'm only in one small area of it. I'm thinking he found people while he was deployed. That or Stanley made the call and found people to fill the open spots. We all know that Stanley and Abbott have been close for years. The dossier that dad had on you, Uncle, had them working together even back then."

"I can't remember a time that Stanley and Abbott didn't work together, but Stanley has always been over him. He makes the calls, gives the orders, and so on," replies Uncle Paul.

"Nobody has approached you about the drive still?" Xander asks as he grabs my hand.

"No, and it wouldn't matter now because we destroyed it. We destroyed it once we looked at the items on it and determined they were all the same items we found separately that showed they were covering up our dad's death."

"Emme, I want you to be very aware of your surroundings at work these next few weeks. I know Abbott hasn't said anything to you, but he's also been gone for several months. You shouldn't have too much interaction with him since he isn't your Commanding Officer any longer, but we also don't know who's working with him right now."

"What did he access, Mav?" Xander asks then takes a sip of his wine.

"Commander Morrison's records."

"As in Emily's Commander Morrison?" inquires Uncle Paul.

Xander coughs practically choking on his wine.

"What was he looking at?" asks Mel.

"I can tell you from what Xander has taught Emme and I, that he accessed Commander Morrison's profile, reviewed current assignments and his direct reports. If I had to guess, he was making sure Emme was still one of them."

"You are not going back to work on Monday. Fake an illness, say you have a family emergency, or whatever you choose, but I think it's safe to say that you should avoid the station once Abbott returns." Xander looks at me pleadingly.

"I appreciate everyone's concern, but he accessed my Commanding Officers' records, he didn't plant a bomb."

"That we know of, Ems."

"Xander, you know I love you and appreciate your concern but I'm going to be fine. He isn't going to do anything at the station. Hell, if anything, I'm safer there than at our house."

"That's comforting thanks for that, my love."

Uncle Paul clears his throat to get us back on track, "How about we let Maverick and Emily watch him for a bit. See what he does and maybe who he's talking to now. He might even lead you to the new muscle that he or Stanley recruited."

I see Xander shoot Maverick one of his looks that says to not let me do this.

"Emme is right Xander, she's safer at the base compared to anywhere else."

"We are upping our security system at the house tomorrow," Xander adamantly replies.

"Thanks for the heads up, Mav. I'll be on alert and keep an ear out. Now can we please get back to dinner before it gets cold?"

"I'm with Emily on this one. I was staring down that dessert we brought the entire ride here, hurry up and eat ya'll this momma doesn't have many uninterrupted dinners anymore."

Mel always knows how to lighten the mood with her sweet southern charm.

"Mel, how are you feeling and how was Evelyn's appointment?" Uncle Paul asks.

"I'm tired all the time but little miss over there has finally started sleeping through the night so that is starting to help. Her appointment went great, she is a healthy happy baby."

We all go back to eating and making small talk about my niece and their plans while they are here for a few days. Once dinner is over, the men grab our dishes and start to clean the kitchen as Mel and I bring out the cake and ice cream for dessert.

After dessert, we finish the night with a card game and say our goodbyes to everyone as Xander and I head back to our house down the street.

EMILY

As we walk back up the stairs and into the Fallon family home, Xander brings up the security system again that he mentioned briefly over dinner.

"I was serious, Ems; I would feel better if we added some upgrades to this house now that Abbott is back on solid ground."

"Awe, babe, I'll protect you," I tell him as I hug him.

"Cute, real cute. Would you please humor me on this? It won't take much; I can install a few exterior cameras around the property and maybe install some sensors on the doors and windows."

My dad always told me to pick my battles and this isn't one that I'm willing to start.

"If you will feel better having those items, I am fine with you installing them or having someone do it for us."

"Thank you, I will look at the options tomorrow."

Xander looks down at me, pulling me to him to embrace me in a hug. He pulls back enough to lean down to kiss me. Every kiss still sends tingles down to my toes. Goosebumps appear on my skin as he deepens the kiss while walking me toward the stairs that lead up to our room. I put my hands on his chest to stop him briefly.

"Why don't we take this outside? We haven't christened the hot tub that we had installed, yet," I say as I wink at him.

The light blue in his eyes instantly changes into the deepest of blues I've ever seen. I've clearly said something he likes.

"Ems, I'm pretty sure I couldn't love you any more than I already do, but comments like that, really help."

"Will you give me ten minutes to put the food away and grab us some fresh wine?"

"I'll go grab some towels and get the cover taken off the tub. Don't be long," he whispers as he pulls me in for another deep kiss.

As Xander heads up to our room to grab some towels and change, I put the food away. I wait for him to head outside before running up to grab my work computer to quickly check the site to see what ships are scheduled to be in this weekend. There is only one and it got here thirty minutes ago, which means Abbott is back. I close my laptop and throw it back in my work bag. Running over to the dresser, I grab Xander's favorite two-piece suit and quickly throw it on. It won't be on long, but I need something to wear outside. I throw my hair into a quick bun and make one more stop at my closet. I open the small access door and use my fingerprint to open my safe. Grabbing my gun, I insert the magazine and pull back the slide to have one ready to go. I'm not taking any chances this time. Walking back into our room, I open the nightstand drawer and place the gun in there for now. I quickly run back down to the kitchen, pour the promised fresh wine, and head out to the hot tub.

The air is a little chilly compared to earlier this evening

but feels refreshing once in the hot tub. Xander's eyes roam over my body as I slowly enter the hot tub.

"I hope you weren't planning to keep that suit on. While I appreciate the effort of you putting it on, it's just in the way."

My suit finds itself on the floor of the patio pretty quickly as Xander makes good on his promise to christen the hot tub.

* * *

I wake up the next morning to the alarm on my phone going off. It's still dark in our room so I'm not sure why it is already going off. I reach over to see if Xander might know and the space next to me is empty.

"Xander?"

He walks into our room dressed in running clothes.

"Going somewhere before the sun is even up?"

"We are going somewhere. When was the last time we ran up to the beach to watch the sunrise?"

"Years I guess, but why today, Xander?"

"Why not today, get dressed, Ems, I want to watch the sunrise with you."

Xander turns and leaves the room.

I grumble briefly but throw back the covers, proceed to the bathroom to change into running clothes, and then I head down the stairs where Xander is waiting with the keys to Katniss.

"Why do you have the keys to Katniss?"

"Because I woke you up early, I thought it would only be fair to drive her over to that cute bagel shop you love so after our run, we can grab some breakfast and head back here. Also, there isn't a direct route to the ocean from here. We can start our run from that parking lot and not worry about running on the bypass while it's still dark out."

"You have thought of everything and thank you because my brain is accustomed to at least one more hour of sleep. I am however awake enough to know that you still aren't driving her."

Xander begrudgingly hands over her keys and we head to the garage and off to park Katniss.

It's dark and very still this early in the morning as we pull into the lot to park the Bronco. I tuck the keys into one of my pockets and start to stretch a bit to wake up my body. From this lot to the beach is a quick mile and a half run, three miles round trip. Xander might be onto something here. I can't remember the last sunrise I got to witness here with him.

"Ready to go?"

"Let's do this, you owe me a bagel and a very large coffee."

"That's why we parked where we did. Now let's go."

We take off at a steady pace, I do love that Xander enjoys running with me now. We turn out of the parking lot and down a road that leads into a tucked-away little neighborhood. Most of these houses have been here for years, yet you will see a few new ones being built throughout the neighborhood as well. We cross over a small bridge that stretches over the creek and continues toward the road that heads to one of the private beaches.

It's a quick fifteen-minute run as we wait at the light to cross the beach road and up the sidewalk toward the small deck that allows access to the beach.

I slide off my shoes to avoid running back with them filled with sand and set them on the railing. Xander does the same and then grabs my hand to walk down onto the beach. He directs me over to a blanket that is set out already.

I look around to see if anyone else is here, but the entire beach is empty or the parts that I can see anyway because the sun isn't up yet.

"Did you put this here?"

"I did, I snuck out a little early."

We sit down on the blanket to take in the sounds of the ocean. The way it ebbs and flows could soothe me right back to sleep. I scoot over close to Xander and lean my head on his shoulder.

"Thanks for waking me up to do this, I've missed moments like this being gone over the past several years."

Xander slides out a bit and turns toward me, grabbing my hands.

"Ems, you are the most important person in my life from the moment you walked into it. Your strawberry blonde hair was tucked into that baseball cap of your dad's playing at this very beach with your brothers when you were five. I remember walking over to you and asking if you wanted to play and we became inseparable from that moment on."

"I want to watch all the sunrises and sunsets with you. I want to create new moments and continue to cherish all of our old ones. You make me crazy at times but in the best way possible. When you aren't near me it feels like a part of me is missing. You accept every piece of me. We have developed our own language over the years that only we understand. One look from you and I know everything you are thinking. The strength and love you have for your family and others is unparalleled. You have always been this beacon of love and inspiration."

"You motivate me, encourage me, and love me like no one else ever has. I can't imagine my life without you and last year when I thought you were taken from me, I knew I didn't want to spend another minute without you knowing how I truly felt about you. I will spend the rest of our days together making sure you know how much I love you. Emily Renee Fallon, will you marry me?"

The sun is beginning to rise and the waves continue to crash calmly against the shore. Xander presents a small box to me. With my eyes full of tears from the incredible proposal he gave I glance at the box and see my mother's wedding band. The one that was in Maverick's safe last year. I look up at Xander and start to cry even harder as I launch myself from my seated position to hug him and almost tackle him to the ground while planting kisses all over his face.

"Yes, I will marry you, Xander Ellis!"

He takes the ring from its cushioned box and places it on my left ring finger. Both of our hands are shaking from the pure excitement we are feeling.

"When we found this last year in Maverick's safe, I made a mental note to ask him about it. He told me the letter that was addressed to him from your mom was about this ring. She wanted him to keep it until I came to my senses and asked you to marry me."

I laugh through my happy tears at the thought of my mom knowing this was how it would be. He picks me up and spins me around hugging me so tightly, like he's afraid to let go.

"She always did love you and thought of you as family. I guess everyone did see how much you loved me before I did. I'm sorry it took me so long, but I promise to continue to make up for the lost time."

He sets me back on the ground. I raise my head to kiss Xander pulling him to me. He deepens the kiss but then pulls back a bit to smile at me before kissing my forehead.

"Before this goes where I hope it does, you might want to wait until we get back to the house." He points back to the deck that we came down from.

There looking down at us and smiling are Maverick, Mel, Evelyn, and Uncle Paul. I kiss his cheek then run over to them.

Mel is crying and Maverick has this *I told you so look* on his face. I think Uncle Paul even has a few tears in his eyes.

They all take turns congratulating and hugging us.

"This is really why we stayed last night. Xander wanted our family here to share this moment with you all," Maverick tells me.

I carefully grab my niece from Mel's arms and tell her that she will be the most beautiful flower girl.

"Already making wedding plans?" Mel laughs.

"Of course, I am! I've wasted so much time not seeing what was right in front of me, why waste anymore? Other than Xander's parents these are all the guests I want at our ceremony. Keep it small and simple with a small reception for friends and family after."

"You really are planning this already," Xander chuckles as he pulls me closer to him.

We climb up the steps to the deck to put our shoes back on as Mel and I continue chatting about wedding plans. Maverick leans in to whisper that mom and dad would be so happy right now. I stretch up onto my toes, grab him to hug him, and thank him for always being here for me. Xander runs back to the sand to grab the blanket and ring box and joins us on the deck.

"Anyone up for some breakfast?" asks Uncle Paul.

We all look at each other and nod.

"We parked over in the lot across the street that's tucked into the trees, that way you wouldn't see us here when you ran by," Maverick tells me.

With my arm around Xander's waist, I squeeze him and tell him that he thought of everything to surprise me in the best way. We follow everyone down the walkway and across the street to their waiting cars. We climb in with Uncle Paul and head back to the little bagel shop where Katniss is parked to have some breakfast with my family and now my fiancé.

SPENCER

Thirty minutes earlier.

I get back in my car while it's still dark out. The sun is set to rise shortly. This assignment has been exhausting. We've been following and monitoring the Fallons for weeks. When Abbott approached me at the station a few months back, he mentioned that there would be lots of downtime. This wasn't what I had in mind when I joined the Navy but when he dangled a ridiculous payday in front of me if I played my cards right, how could I turn it down? It was supposed to be me and this other guy Pierce who would keep an eye on the family. Pierce is pretty cool but keeps to himself.

We were told to report any findings back to Abbott directly. At first, we would follow them together and do stakeouts, but we felt we were missing something. Pierce suggested splitting off into twelve-hour shifts. Last night the Fallons had their family dinner. Two days before they usually do. When I told Pierce that, he mentioned that he thinks they might be planning something. I offered to take a few hours from his morning shift to see what else might happen.

While I was watching the house this morning, I saw their bedroom light turn on pretty early. Even for the redhead. She's a robot usually waking up around 6:00 a.m. to go for a run, but today it was much earlier. Plus, the guy left around 4:30 this morning. Maybe I should have followed him but he isn't the main concern now. He wasn't gone long so he couldn't have gone too far.

I watch the shadows behind the blinds of her bedroom window. I have her outline memorized. She's very athletic, with her toned body. Her porcelain skin and reddish hair fits her. Shaking my head to get my mind right for the assignment, I hear the garage door open. I slide down in my seat to hopefully avoid being seen as they drive by. After a minute, I turn the truck on and follow them.

They park in a strip mall parking lot. All the stores and restaurants are still closed because it's barely dawn. I continue to the stoplight in front of me while watching them in my rearview mirror. They both exit the car and the girl begins to stretch. My assessment was correct, they are going for a run. Over the past few months, they have gone a handful of different routes. But from this location only one place makes sense. The beach is a mile up if you run through a neighborhood that sits behind the businesses.

Once the light turns green, I turn down the street that leads to the beach. I glance over and see them heading in my direction. I need to find a place to park quickly with the hope of intercepting them. Their typical route through this neighborhood ends with them at the beach. I quickly scan the houses for one that is vacant. Up to the right, I see a rental home that's listed for sale. It has a three-level deck off the back of the house. Perfect height to see over the tree line and directly down to them. They could turn off onto a different road but I have a feeling they are up this early to catch the sunrise. I pull the truck into the drive and wait a few minutes.

When I feel enough time has passed for them to catch up to me, I get out and walk to the back of my truck, I hear the cadence of a runner. Maybe it's another person out this early. I stop to listen and make out that it's two runners, not one. Before grabbing my case from the back of my truck, I look over my shoulder to see that they have caught up to my location. This will be the first time I see them up close without a telephoto lens.

At the same time, I look over, she turns her head in my direction and smiles. That smile lights up her whole face even though it's still dark out. It's like I'm seeing her for the first time. The past few weeks she's been nothing more than a target to watch and observe. But that smile that she gave me was deliberately meant for me. I'm conflicted now as to how I should proceed. Do I protect her now or follow my orders? The thought of her as something more than a mark piques my interest. The confusion awakens a feeling in my loins. Nobody can protect her like I can.

Their steady pace has them almost to the end of the road. Grabbing my case from the back of the truck, I head inside, breaking the spell her smile briefly put me under.

After a few minutes of setting up my equipment, I look through my scope and spot her and the guy sitting on the beach. Perfect timing. It appears he just proposed. The guy points behind them and I notice the other members of her family standing on the deck that is used to access the beach. They must have gotten there while I was setting it up. I need to focus. Shaking my head to clear it, I look back into the scope.

The Fallon family is walking down the sidewalk and is about to cross back over the beach road. The thrill of watching her from a distance allows me to immerse myself in her world. She's so close but blissfully unaware. I could spend countless hours thinking about different ways to eliminate those who could come between us. Her friends, family, and co-workers; they're all insignificant. Our connection is real and unmatched compared to the others in her life.

I look through my scope and put her in the center of it first to get a close-up view as my phone starts to vibrate in my pocket. She's laughing and appears to be happy. If she only knew I could make her even happier. Not sure what someone like her did to deserve a target on her back.

"Yep?"

"What are you doing?"

"Sir, I'm observing the family as you ordered, Sir. I can take some of the family out now if you would like. I have them in my site."

"Stand down and that's an order. You are relatively new to this group so I'm going to explain a few things. Listen up, because I won't repeat myself. You only take out a target when ordered to. Your current assignment is recon. Since you missed your first day at boot camp when that term was covered, it means to observe and collect intel. You will not go rogue like your predecessors. Am I making myself clear?"

"Crystal, Sir."

"Lastly, you are not the only one doing the watching. You are also being watched because you haven't proven yourself to me and neither has that dipshit, Pierce. Pack up your kit and get back to collecting intel. I will be in touch."

"Sir, yes Sir."

The call ends and I start to pack up my things. I walk down the spiral staircase that leads back to the main deck. I go back through the rental house like I came in and watch through the window as I see their cars exit the tree-covered parking lot. Once I'm confident they have gone, I proceed out to my truck to stow my case and head back to the house being provided for Pierce and I on this group of islands.

The boss wants us close enough to collect intel on the Fallons and not spend wasted time driving between the station and here. It makes sense to have us close so we blend in with their community and not stand out. Enemies closer and all that.

I pull out of the drive and head back to the house just off the bypass.

"You get anything today?" Pierce asks as I walk through the front door.

"Not really and did you know we are being watched?"

"I didn't, but I get it. I heard the last two assholes that worked for this group massively fucked up. That's why we got brought in, to clean up their mess."

"Whatever, I'm going to bed, it's your turn to babysit the Fallons. I clocked them at the bagel shop across from here. Shouldn't be hard to miss with that blue jeep that the girl drives."

"On it, Spencer. I'll let you know if anything interesting happens. Oh, and you got a package delivered earlier today it's on the kitchen counter."

Pierce leaves to start his rotation of Fallon babysitting. It's a Saturday so maybe it will be uneventful for him. I mean, they already got their run out of the way, and looks like they got engaged as well. The lucky bastard might not even have to leave their neighborhood today.

I grab myself something quick to eat before trying to wind down and catch a few hours of sleep before my rotation starts again. Sitting down at the kitchen counter with some leftover Chinese food, I reach for the package Pierce put on the counter. No return address or identifying markings. I open the large envelope and drop out the contents onto the counter. There are some surveillance photos of me and two trackers with a typed note:

We are always watching and the trackers are for you to use as you see fit with the Fallons.

Thinking to myself, *whatever man*, I slide the contents over and grab my camera to look at the photos I've taken over the past few days.

Several of them are of her and the guy she's now engaged to. When she's not at work, they are always together. I need to find a time when they aren't together, maybe try to talk to her or accidentally run into her.

Continuing to flip through the photos, I see I've captured a blast of them from almost every angle. One of them is when I caught her standing in front of her window. She thought she was alone. Looking at the photo gives me a bit of a rush. Remembering the way she moves or how she talks to people is intoxicating.

She's very easy to look at, especially in these shots from when they were in the hot tub last night. There's almost a magnetic force drawing me to her. I've studied her movements and every interaction she's had the past several days. Last night it should have been me that was giving it to her in that hot tub, hell maybe that's what I'll do when I get her alone. She should know that we are meant to be together.

I toss the remaining cold Chinese food away and go to take a cold shower. I'm never gonna sleep if I keep thinking about her in that hot tub.

ABBOTT

Eleven Years Earlier- 2008

The air is crisp this early in the morning on the ship. The ocean is calm and, in some areas, looks like glass until the Navy Destroyer cuts through it to get to its destination. Heading to Ecuador to check in on the seals is a quick turnaround. This mission is a bit different from the others. Stanley and I have been working with the Cartel for a while now and things were going smoothly until Mike Fallon stuck his damn nose into our operation. Getting rid of Paul was easy, Stanley had him discharged from the Navy in order to keep him out of our business. From what I can tell after I followed Paul when he met up with Mike, he must have spilled everything about our little side missions. Mike has been snooping around the station and now this ship all week, he's been seen in parts of this ship he doesn't need to be in. He must really think we're dumb if he thinks we're keeping drugs or anything like that on board.

I head to the war room to have a brief meeting with Stanley.

"Close the door, Abbott."

After closing the door, I turn to face him waiting for him to speak.

"There's rumored to be a DEA agent snooping around now. My understanding is that Mike Fallon has something to do with that."

As he continues to go on about his suspicions, I notice him messing with something in his hand. He keeps flipping something repeatedly.

"Are you still carrying around that rook chess piece after all these years?"

"Yes, I do."

"Is there some significance with that piece? Did it save your life?"

"It's a constant reminder for me."

"A reminder of what?"

"This piece, the rook, is one of the most powerful pieces in the game of chess. But not the most powerful piece. That would be the King and then the Queen. It's a reminder that while I have a powerful role, there is someone else who is at a higher level that I answer to. For now. To me, chess is like life. It can be a very short game if you know what you are doing and you are a stronger player compared to your opponent. Or it can be a long game. You do as expected, toe the line, and maybe you will live a long life and come out on the other end unscathed."

"You're a control freak got it. Now why am I here?"

"Before you interrupted me, I was explaining that the DEA is now looking into our operation and we believe that Mike Fallon is responsible. Whatever you have planned for him, it needs to happen soon."

"I already told you it will be handled on this trip."

"I'm holding you to that."

"Anything else, Stanley?"

STORM FROM WITHIN

"If I'm the rook, that makes you a pawn. Don't fuck this up or I will remove you from the board."

"Don't threaten me, Stanley. We go back a long time. I know all your secrets."

"Nobody knows all of my secrets."

With that last comment I leave the room and head back to the bridge to get my mind right for today.

The operation for Em-Comm, Ecuador Movement Command, only requires us to look the other way while the Cartel makes its drug runs. We provide the travel routes for our ships and the Coast Guard so they can avoid being intercepted by us. Once every few trips we happen to catch a low-level runner to make it look like we're still upholding our end of the deal with Ecuador, which is to help stop the drug trafficking and smuggling business in and around their ports.

This trip is different though, Stanley wants me to permanently remove Fallon from the situation as he feels he's getting too close to the truth and Stanley isn't ready to let this funnel of income go yet. Being in the Navy pays like every other government job, not enough. Stanley trusts me to arrange meetings and check on the side business while I'm here and now this new task is one more thing I get to deal with. I need to figure out how that's going to happen. Crew members disappear at sea all the time, I could make it look like an accident. Maybe I can have one of the Cartel guys take care of him. I need to have people see him on this ship before and after the regular mission, though, so that won't work.

As we near the port, I put the thoughts about offing Fallon to the back of my mind.

"Sir, here is the itinerary for our week here," says Lieutenant Smith as he hands me a folder of dates and times for training and meetings with the seals.

"Thank you, Lieutenant Smith." Taking the folder, I flip through the itinerary and see what is planned for our short time here as I head back to my quarters to grab some items before we officially dock.

Everyone's been given their assignments prior to today so everything should run smoothly without much involvement from me for a few hours. I need to sneak away to meet with the Cartel contact. Stanley was the one to meet with them before but now he's an Admiral and can't get away as easily as I can.

On my way there I stop at a little market to grab a few items for the ship, that's when I see her. I never wanted to get involved with anyone after my first wife died. I figured it was the penance I was owed for being a criminal while wearing this uniform. A life of solitude and I had come to terms with that until I see her. Her long dark brown hair and light brown eyes search my face when we run into each other in this small market near Manta, Ecuador. She looks so flustered while trying to find words to apologize. I guess the uniform throws her off and she thinks she will be in trouble but quite the opposite. Bending down to pick up the items she dropped, I help her carry them to the cashier. By the time she pays for her items, I'm trying my damnedest to speak the very little Spanish I know to find out how to see her again. I must have said something funny because she's shaking her head and giggling at my last comment. She raises her eyes to meet mine and her cheeks are tinged with pink but she agrees to meet me at this same market tomorrow.

The next day after the daily exercises with both Navies and a ship tour with the Mayor of Manta, I had another quick meeting with the Cartel. One of our trusted contacts has already been informed about the situation at hand with Fallon. He gives me some of his precious cargo laced with something that would make Fallon's heart stop within seconds. All I have to do is get him to ingest it and then throw him overboard while making it look like an accident. The Cartel would then step in, grab his body, and make it disappear for good. They have our travel routes so they know roughly where he will end up based on the coordinates. Easier said than done but it needs to happen, he's a liability and needs to be handled.

After meeting with our contact, I hurry back to the market from yesterday. Three days at port isn't nearly enough time to get to know her. I find out that her name is Maria and she's a few years younger than I am. The language barrier is still a bit rough but I try to convey that I don't want to leave so soon but I have to. I ask her to write to me and give her my address and phone number if she would need anything. I also try to explain that I'm not here but a few times a year she doesn't seem to mind as she walks closer to me and puts her hand on my arm. She loops her arm through mine and nudges me out of the market. We walk toward a building of small apartments and head into a stairwell that travels up two flights. Her apartment is up the stairs and to the right. Once inside she offers me a drink and attempts a few words in English.

"You hungry? Food?"

"I'm fine but thank you. You speak English?"

She makes a gesture with her fingers that translates to very little.

I walk to her and grab her hands. "I don't know how to make this work but something in me tells me I need to try. I have this pulling feeling that I need to know everything about you and even though I don't know anything about you except your name, I feel I've known you for years. Once I leave, I feel like a piece of me will be missing."

She leans towards me and places her head on my chest.

I didn't see this happening while I was here this time. It's a complication for sure but one I'm going to figure out, I have this urge to protect her and even with the language barrier, I know she has the same feeling.

After a few hours of us trying to teach each other the other's language, I decide it's time to say our goodbyes. I tell her I won't be back the next day as it's a full day of training and then preparing for our departure. I won't be able to sneak away. She stands up from the chair she is in and reaches for my hand to have me do the same. Looking down at her I can see the hurt on her face that I'm leaving, and she doesn't know when I'll be back. I kiss her once to try to express the fact that I don't want to leave but I have to. She deepens the kiss. *God what am I doing?* I think to myself while she walks me to her small bedroom. She takes off her dress and stands before me, this vision of perfection. I don't deserve her; my remaining years were meant to be alone after all I've done and will continue to do after making a deal with the Devil.

I put my hands on her shoulders and the look I try to convey is that we don't need to do this because I know I won't be back for a long while. She starts to unbutton my shirt and then my pants. She traces her hands down the scars on my chest that were from prior missions. She kisses them as if trying to heal them from the touch of her lips. I pick her up and carry her to her bed, laying her down gently, I look at her one more time trying to give her an out. The passion in her eyes is all I need to ravage her body.

An hour later, I slip out from her apartment while she peacefully sleeps. I wrote her a note in English and attempt to translate it into Spanish letting her know I will be back as soon as I can, but it might be up to a year.

After my meeting with our contact, observing the

training exercises, and making one other stop, I'm finally heading back to the ship. It's nearing the end of our last day in Ecuador. The sun is starting to set as the crew prepares for our departure. As I get closer to the port my phone starts to ring.

"What?"

"Why is he still snooping around? I thought you were handling the situation," the metallic cold voice slices into my eardrum.

"I've been overseeing drills and slipping away to meet with our contact who was generous enough to provide a bit of assurance in powder form."

"That's not all you slipped away to do," he says with disdain.

"Now you're having me followed?"

"I can't take any chances, I already had to cut someone who I thought could handle this influx of cash but the pressure got to him. Do I need to remove you and Fallon from the situation or do you think you can finish the mission you were assigned?"

"I'm getting back on the ship now. It will be done this evening."

"Handle it or it becomes a two-for-one kind of night."

"Understood."

The call ends and I have to restrain myself from launching my cell phone into the ocean.

As I get back on the ship, I think through the main assignment I was given for this trip and that's to remove Fallon. We have been told that he's been talking to others and found out about our agreement. He's been following us or having us followed and now he's been snooping around the entire time we've been traveling here. My hand gravitates to my pocket, and I feel for the small package of white powder that is intended for my target.

The sun has disappeared for the day and the moon is covered by a never-ending cloud bank making it eerily dark on the deck of the ship. While a quarter of the crew is in the mess for dinner and the remainder is either manning the ship, taking inventory, or preparing for our departure, I ask Mike to discuss his thoughts on an upcoming mission. He doesn't know that I know he's been looking into our plans. He meets me on the deck near the bridge but within a blind spot keeping us undetected. I hand him a cup of coffee laced with the package from earlier. With it being chilly out this evening he doesn't think twice, as he grabs the cup and starts to drink. I've heard that cocaine is tasteless when mixed with something acidic like coffee. I have also heard that the caffeine from coffee mixed with cocaine can increase your heart rate and blood pressure, the extra additive from our local drug dealer doesn't hurt to ensure the task is handled quickly.

"Have you put any thought into this next mission?" I ask him.

"I've been reviewing the notes and the schematics but not much past that. You?"

With his coffee a quarter of the way gone, Mike starts to cough a bit. I keep looking out to sea drinking my coffee and ignoring his question. The coughing turns into a gurgle from the choking the chemical combo is causing. That stuff really does work fast.

He leans over the edge of the ship to try and get a good breath, I set down my coffee before lifting his legs to push him over helping him to slip into the void of the ocean. It's dark enough out and with the wake the ship creates, he is gone.

I lean down to grab my coffee from the deck, take another sip, and look up toward the bridge noticing that nobody is any the wiser about what happened. There aren't too many minutes on this ship without someone else around, this happened to be a few of them. I sip my coffee and head back to the war room to finish out my evening knowing my contact will be picking up Fallon's body and taking care of disposal.

The next day operations and exercises aboard go on as planned, it isn't until late the following evening that someone asks about Mike. The word spreads quicker on a ship than teenage girls gossiping. I order the helmsman to slow the ship and sound an alert to have everyone start searching. I also ask for the Coast Guard and Air Force to be called to assist with a possible search and rescue in case he fell overboard. I have to keep up appearances, right? I hope our Cartel friends took care of the situation before they started their search and rescue efforts.

After several days of joint efforts, we decided to continue our journey home. Mike Fallon has not been located at this time and is being considered MIA.

XANDER

Present Day

As we finish breakfast with the family and say our goodbyes, I can't help but notice the cheesy smile on my girl's face. I would marry her today if it were up to me, but I'm going to follow her lead.

"Xander, thank you so much for all of this. I couldn't have dreamt of a better proposal. The first place we met, with my family, and my mom's wedding ring. Even my face hurts from smiling so much," Ems says with a laugh.

Before we get into the vehicle, I pull her in for a hug and slowly walk her backward until her back is up against the bronco. I constantly want to hold her after everything that happened last year. I won't tell her but I still have nightmares of the gunshot and not knowing if it was her or Asher. A few strands have fallen from her hair after being up earlier and she's never looked more gorgeous. I move them behind her ear as she leans her face into my hand.

"Ems, how many times do I have to tell you? I will do

anything for you and I will spend our remaining days showing you and telling you how much I love you."

"Maybe we should go home so you can show me how much you love me."

"Why go home? There's plenty of room in here," I ask as I tap on the vehicle.

She laughs and pushes me away from her to get in and we head the few minutes back to the house.

"What's the plan for today?"

"Well first, I'm going to make good on that promise I made about showing you how much I love you. Then I thought we would go ahead and get the extra security items I mentioned last night at dinner. I'm not letting that go. Followed by any shopping you want to do before you go back to work on Monday."

"Xander, life lesson, never tell a woman she can do any shopping she wants. I promise you will regret that comment by the end of the day."

We pull into the garage and I chase her up the stairs to our room. I don't even let her get undressed, I pull her into the bathroom and then the shower fully clothed.

"It's much more fun when I get to take your clothes off and you need a shower anyways. Hey, I'm trying to save time and money so you have more of both for shopping."

The water hasn't warmed up yet so she squeals a little and laughs. Her laugh is something I could recognize anywhere. Pure perfection.

….

After I thoroughly wash her... twice, we finally decide to leave the bathroom and get dressed to head out the door.

"Where are we going for these much-needed items?"

"Head down the bypass, there's a tech store near Kill Devil Hills close to that family-owned bookstore you loved when you were in college. I can get everything we need from there. After that, the day is yours, my love."

"Is that bookstore still there?"

"Sadly no, the owner passed away a few years ago and the remaining family members decided to close up shop. The new owners turned it into a jewelry store."

"I think I know where I want to go after you get this security business out of your system."

"I know we've been engaged for only a few hours, but have you had any thoughts on what you would like to do for the wedding, Ems?"

"Xander, most women spend their entire childhood planning out the perfect wedding. I'm not one of those women though. I feel like you can spend all that time planning but who's to say your partner wants the same thing? Here's what I know right now at this moment, I love you so much and I would be fine getting married today. I don't need a drawn-out engagement. All I want is you. I was telling Mel this earlier, a small ceremony on the beach in a few months with the same people that were at the beach this morning and of course your parents would be perfect. We can plan a big reception for all our friends and extended family after that. What do you think about that as a plan?"

"I think that sounds perfect. We should look into obtaining the marriage license and finding someone to perform the ceremony. From there, I think we can do whatever feels right."

She pulls into the parking lot and we walk into the security store to grab a few new additions for the house. An hour later, I walk out with three new cameras and enough window and door sensors for the entire house plus a panel to set an alarm based on areas of the house. After placing the newly acquired items into the back of Katniss, I turn towards Ems and extend my hand for hers. She grabs it and has this smile that reaches her eyes as we head down the shopping center's sidewalk toward the jewelry store.

"Is there something specific you want to look for?"

"I wanted to pick out your band, I have something in mind so I'm wondering if it can either be made or if they already have it as an option."

I open the door for her and follow her into the jewelry store.

"Good afternoon, folks, how may I help you today?" asks the jeweler.

"I wanted to look at wedding bands for my fiancé."

"Of course, my dear, right this way."

The jeweler walks us toward one of the back counters. Inside the glass, there are rows of men's rings.

"These are all our ring options for men but they are displays only. If you find one that speaks to you, we can have it ordered and received quickly. When is the big day?"

"We are still working on that part but likely in the next few months over the summer," I tell him while looking down at Ems.

She takes her time looking from row to row. I can tell something catches her eye as she lets out an audible breath.

"May I see that one? Although the one that incorporated the bullets is interesting." She winks at me.

"Too soon, Ems."

"You have a great eye, my dear. This metal is tantalum, it's the strongest one available. It's a little pricey but worth it because it's scratch-resistant, shatterproof, and overall, a low-maintenance metal. A little fun fact, this particular metal is what they make jet engines out of due to the high heat resistance, so they are very durable. If you are an active person or work with your hands a lot, this would be an excellent ring to go with."

It takes me everything to not comment on that last part. Em sees me smirk out of the corner of her eye and playfully smacks my arm. She takes the ring and looks closer at it. "How is this compared to tungsten or titanium?"

"All three are excellent metals each with their distinct qualities. Tungsten is a bit heavier, and titanium is lighter but neither of them holds up against the tantalum. Would you like to see a few more?"

"No, this is the one I want." She hands him back the tantalum ring.

"I'll put the order in now and call you when it's ready for pick up. We offer to engrave if you would like to add that as well before it ships."

"Yes, I would like to have it engraved."

The jeweler hands her a pen and a form to fill out.

"Excuse me, sir, do you have that exact band but for ladies?"

"Yes sir, I believe I do. Right over here."

I follow the jeweler to a different display case as he unlocks it to grab the requested ring. He hands it to me to inspect.

"Please add a separate order for this one and I would also like to have it engraved."

"Fill this out and I will get you both checked out then have these sent off for engraving."

"Xander, you stay over there, please? You already get to see the ring I'm getting you and I know that's my fault, but I would like one small surprise for our wedding day."

"Back at ya, Ems."

I nod in agreement and walk to the other end of the store as Ems writes something down on the purchase form for the ring. I see the jeweler smile and finish ringing her up. Ems pays for the ring and heads back toward me. Wrapping her arms around me she looks up and smiles. I release her, hand the jeweler my request and my credit card. Once the transactions are complete, we head to the door and back out to vehicle.

"Anything else you want to check off the wedding planning list today while we are out?" I ask her.

"I know it's been a while since we've spent the day shopping, but that actually sounds terrible. If you want to shop more, I'm sure I can think of something. All I care about now is your parents being here with the family and having a ring to give you on our day. We just need to figure out the marriage license and find someone to marry us. We can wear sweats on our wedding day I don't even care about a dress."

"Ems, it's going to be summertime, can we not wear sweats?"

She laughs and drives us back to the house. I warn her that for the remainder of the afternoon I will be installing our new security items if she's sure there's nothing else she wants to shop for or look at.

"I know that's important to you so you work on that and I will do some research into the license and people to marry us."

I squeeze her hand as we get closer to the house.

Once we are in the garage, I grab the new security items from the back, kiss her on her check and head to the living room to start figuring out where to start.

"Let me know if you need anything, this will keep me busy for a few hours."

She tells me not to worry as she heads up to our room to do some research.

There's a knock at the door, but by the time I get to it, nobody is there. Looking around I don't see anyone walking away. When I look down, I notice an envelope.

Not again, I think to myself. My name is on it unlike the

ones we received last year that were blank. I open the envelope to see a typed note.

Xander, you don't know me but I have intel on Mike's murder. Check your email for more information. Don't tell anyone.

What the hell is this about? Last year all of the envelopes were from Uncle Paul. I know he didn't send this or bring this over. Is this Abbott's new game? It can't be, he wouldn't resort to this. He's more of a shoot first, deal with it later kind of guy from what I've gathered.

For now, I put the envelope in my office and under my laptop. I'll do what it says and wait for an email to see what it has to say before I do anything.

ABBOTT

*E*ight years earlier- 2011

I get back to my beach house in Kill Devil Hills after checking my mailbox at the local post office. It's become a frequent routine for me every few months after visiting Ecuador. I've had to get creative with my last few visits there. Two years ago, Stanley told me he had me followed so now I make sure to cover my tracks and double back before meeting up with Maria. I don't want anyone to find out about her and whatever I can do to protect her, I'm going to do it.

We've been writing for the past few months and try to make time for calls on the weekends, when I'm home. There's a new letter. Opening the envelope a few photos fall out of it that are of my son. Maria told me on one of our calls a few months after I left that she was pregnant. While there was still a bit of a language barrier her English and my Spanish had improved dramatically from that first run in. Between talking on the phone and writing letters, we were both starting to be more comfortable with communicating. When she told me she was pregnant it was clear as day all those months ago.

"Theodore, you are going to be a father."

I sat down as the wind left my chest; did I hear her correctly?

"Maria, did you say I'm going to be a father?"

"Yes! Yes, my love, you have given me such a beautiful gift. I'm two months pregnant now, maybe on your next trip here, you will get to meet your child."

Even though Maria wanted to name him after me, she allowed me to pick his first name, so I went with my favorite baseball player, Miguel "Miggy" Cabrera. He plays for the Detroit Tigers. She chose his middle name and for safety he has her last name. Miggy, was almost a year old before I met him the first time and it was only briefly on my last deployment to Ecuador. Even with extra precautions, I keep our visits short. Looking at him I can see that he has his mother's eyes, my nose, and so far, her demeanor. I hope that part stays the same. I've never cared about anyone else other than my late wife. While this is all new to me it feels familiar and I will do anything to keep them safe.

I take a few minutes to write her back making sure to not make any promises of me being there anytime soon. The past few months have been rough not seeing them but it is what it is when you walk the line between criminal and Navy Admiral. I let her know that I made a deposit into an account that I had her setup once she told me she was pregnant.

* * *

*2*015

Anytime we were needed in Ecuador, Stanley makes sure my destroyer is the ship sent, not because of Maria and my son because nobody knows about them, but because he knows I can handle the tasks required for our side mission. Once a year my ship makes the quick trip to Ecuador, I make all the required appearances for the Navy and meet up with our Cartel contact to provide the foreseeable coordinates so they can avoid them during their drug smuggling trips. At least once every trip I make time with Maria and our son Miggy who's getting so big. I'm thankful she gave him her last name; she understands it's required for their safety. She doesn't understand all that I do but she knows I'm an American in the Navy and while our nations work together, there's still the ability for things to go sideways.

In 2015, right before Miggy turned four, I was deployed again. I packed a little something to give him for his birthday based off his namesake. After making the required appearances, I wandered around Manta a bit to cover my tracks and to ensure I wasn't being followed before heading to see my family. Maria greeted me like no time had passed at all. She does an amazing job with Miggy, she talks about me all of the time so when I'm here he's very comfortable with me. Not wanting to waste any time, I pulled a package from my bag that I'd been carrying around town that day and handed it to my son to open. His light brown eyes looked up at me with so much excitement as he crawled into my lap. He tore open the paper and said, "Baseball."

"Yes, baseball. You are named after one of the greats, son. You are never too young to learn to play."

He slid from my lap as I started to open the baseball and bat set for him. We spent the next hour playing baseball in Maria's tiny living room.

EMILY

*P*resent Day

With the weekend behind us and the new security system installed, it's time for me to head back to work.

"Xander, can I borrow your car today to take to work?"

"Something wrong with Katniss?"

"She's been acting up a bit and I haven't had time to take care of her. I meant to give her a tune-up this past weekend but with everything you planned, I didn't get around to it and I wouldn't have it any other way," I tell him as I kiss his cheek.

He smiles as he hands me his keys and asks me to follow him into my dad's office. I stop in the doorway for a minute because seeing all of the boxes that now hold my dad's items and our memories are taking me a bit to adjust to. Xander turns to see the look on my face and comes over to hug me.

"I wouldn't have packed anything up if you hadn't told me, you were on board with it. If you want me to put it all back, I will do it right now, Ems."

"No, it's fine, I think it will help me move on a bit. It's always been hard for me to be in this room, my parent's room, and David's room. Seeing the rooms stuck in the past has never really allowed me the closure I needed." I rise to my tiptoes and give him a quick kiss.

He looks into my eyes and once he's satisfied with my response, he walks me around to the other side of the desk. It has two large monitors on it and each monitor has multiple images being displayed. In the bottom corner, I notice that there's a date and time, and all the images are in real time.

"I finished installing all the security items last night after you went to bed but I wanted you to see it before you left today. I don't have cameras in any of our bedrooms but all the windows in those rooms have sensors along with all the doors to the house and the remaining windows throughout the rest of the house. These cameras are mainly for the perimeter of the exterior but this monitor over here does have a few smaller cameras that are providing a feed that is focused on the doors from the inside of the house. Make a mental note, Ems, no frisky business in these select areas because this feed also goes to Maverick."

"God, that would be horrific having him see any of that! While I think you have outdone yourself and maybe have gone a bit overboard, I appreciate all of the hard work," I say with a laugh.

I tell him I'm going to be late as I jingle his keys at him, grab my to-go cup of coffee, and head toward the garage to our vehicles. He waves goodbye as I back out of the garage and he closes the door behind me.

The real reason I'm taking his car is so I can do some recon on Abbott. Now that he's back, I need to see what he's up to. My car stands out too much, Xander's blends in with all the other vehicles that will be at the station. He also doesn't have an official tag so I'll be parking in the visitor lot to hopefully go unnoticed by anyone that might be looking for my vehicle specifically.

I know keeping this from him is going to be a much larger discussion later and I hate hiding it from him but he wouldn't let me go if he knew I planned to do this. Today, I hope to get a feel for what Abbott knows and who he might be working with.

I continue my drive to Norfolk, VA, while I think about where to start because we work in two different areas of the station. There is no reason for me to be over in his area and vice versa so what would put me there? I think to myself for a few minutes. I could tell him I'm looking for the Chief Mate, that's who keeps the ship logs for their trip. That we received an email about some issues that occurred this past trip and I need to review the logs. Yep, that might work as a reason to be over there. Continuing my drive for the next hour, I find parking in the visitor's lot and head into the station. I figure I need to get this over with now so I head toward Abbott's area.

As I get closer to his office, I can see his door open and the light on. He should be off but signs indicate he might be in today. His administrative assistant is either out or away from her desk. I walk past his office and glance back to see if he's even in there. His light is on but his office is empty. Looking around really quickly and in both directions of the hallway, I can see the area is empty. I run into his office and look at his virtually spotless desk. A few sticky notes with nothing of importance on them, his laptop that is closed, a lamp, and a pen/pencil holder are the only items on top of the desk. No personal items whatsoever. I look around the rest of the office, there are a few wooden file cabinets, and some Navy paintings adorning the walls. Otherwise, this office is almost sterile from human interaction. I quickly walk back out the door and look behind me to see that nobody is behind or in front of me as I move toward my area of the station.

Ten minutes later, I enter my office and have a seat behind my desk. I open my work bag and remove my regular work items; my PC, notebook, and work phone. Leaving my navy-issued handgun in the bag in its lockbox but I reach for the tracker I picked up a few weeks earlier when I ran some errands while Xander was over in Manteo doing some repairs to his family home. He is planning to rent it out as an Air B N B for a bit as another source of income. I saw that as an opportunity to get a few things done that might require some answers to questions that I'm not ready to discuss just yet. I palm the tracker that is almost identical to the disc tracker we found on the bronco last year. If he is here, he should be in his usual parking spot, I need to make my way back to the lot and look for his car. Once I place the tracker, it will limit the number of interactions I need to have with him.

Once outside I quickly scan the lot he usually parks in, I see his car almost immediately. I look around the lot and don't see anyone else out right now. I quick step to the row of his vehicle and move towards it. Once I'm near the back passenger tire, I kneel to give the visual of me tying my shoe as I plant the tracker into the wheel well. I stand back up and quickly exit the lane and head back inside to start my actual workday checking my phone in the process to make sure the signal works before abandoning it completely. All is good.

SPENCER

I passed her earlier on her run today and she didn't even seem to notice a new person out at such an early time. Maybe that's typical around here, it is a tourist town after all. Pierce and I have talked about how to approach her, one of us might try to be the guy next door's new neighbor so we can infiltrate their group while the other keeps surveillance. That's one angle for sure. The other option is to continue with our current plan of twelve-hour shifts and maintain our distance for now, which Pierce thinks is best.

Thankfully, the house they put us in isn't far from where she and the guy stay so it allows me time to run home and shower and then resume following her to the station before my shift starts. She left me something today from her run. Her hair tie broke mid-run. She discarded it in the dumpster that was located between us. I went to retrieve it after she passed.

Once I had her gift in my possession, I increased my speed to catch up with her. The guy she's with caught me looking at her a little too long I think when I gave her a small nod and quick smile. A thank you for my present. Oh well, once I have a chance to speak to her, I think she will feel the same connection to me as I do with her. For now, he's simply a placeholder.

Today, I need to plant the tracker while she's at work, that way we can monitor from afar as well. Shit, why is she driving the guy's car today instead of her bronco? Well, I guess that's why the boss probably gave me more than one of these, might as well use them all.

We get to the station and I watch as she continues to the visitor parking lot which makes sense because the car she's driving isn't her usual one. I park in my assigned space for now. I have all day to plant the tracker on the vehicle. Walking inside the station I head toward my Commanders office to see if he's in. After ten minutes of walking, I turn the corner to see her darting into his office. Quickly, I move behind the wall to wait for her.

She takes her time but eventually passes by me as she heads back to her side of the station. I turn away from her and mess with my phone trying to avoid running into her. She discards something in the wastebasket up ahead of me. Once she's around the corner, I head to basket to see what she left for me. I've been collecting small items that she's discarded with the hope to get to know her better. Today it's a coffee cup. After collecting the cup, I can feel the weight of a little substance left behind. Taking a sip, I allow my lips and tongue to linger where hers once were. It's like we are one now. She left this for me. Another gift. Allowing a little trace of her to trickle down inside me. I'll add this new prize to the broken hair tie with a few strands of her hair that she discarded for me near the beach. It still smells like her coconut and vanilla shampoo.

I go back the way I came, deciding that now is not the time to go after her. It's safe to assume that the

Commander isn't in if she was in there. Grabbing for my phone, I make a call to Pierce.

"I'm trying to sleep, what do you want, Spencer?"

"I need you to check out the guy, today, he was at the house when I left for work."

"He isn't part of the problem."

"Yet. He isn't part of the problem, yet. But I'm thinking we can use him. The Boss said he was supposed to be good with computers or some shit."

"Isn't this the exact thing he told you not to do? We should stick to the original plan he gave us. Abbott isn't going to like this."

"We need to prove ourselves, right? Abbott works for Stanley, right? Stanley controls who is in as far as their team is concerned from what I can tell. If we want to move into the inner circle at some point, we need to be resourceful. What if we bring intel on the guy to Abbott and show him that he's an asset and that we can use him. Abbott is happy and maybe tells Stanley. We help him and it helps us in the process. Everybody wins. Well, maybe not the computer guy."

"Whatever, Spencer, I'm going back to bed but if I feel like it, I'll look in on the guy later.

"We need this, Pierce; I'm not taking the long road to get the things I want in this life. If you won't help me, I will do it myself but it would be great if you would get your fucking head out of your ass and help me for once."

"Two hours man, give me two hours more to sleep and I will do your bitch work and check on the guy."

"Was that so hard?"

"Eat a dick, Spencer."

I can't help but laugh at Pierce's comment as I continue toward my office. Maybe the guy will be helpful or maybe

Abbott will want him removed. Either could work in my favor.

After a few hours of work, I head back over to the Commander's office. The lights are out now. Looking down the hall in both directions, I can see the area is clear. I continue into his office to see if anything appears touched or moved but nothing looks out of place from what I can tell. Feeling for the tracker in my back pocket I move toward the visitor parking lot. With it being on the opposite side of the station from where Fallon's office is, she won't see me out there and it isn't her usual lunchtime based on the past few weeks of watching her.

I move quickly to the Nissan she drove today weaving between cars in a bent over almost squat position hoping to not be seen. As I approach the vehicle, I look around to see if anyone else is around; nobody is in the lot. Dropping to the ground quickly, I lay down and slide halfway under the vehicle placing the tracker with the magnet under the vehicle. Most people mistakenly put them in the wheel well and ultimately get caught. Once I'm satisfied with the placement, I check the app on my phone to make sure the signal is working and then head back to my office to finish out my day before heading back to the house.

"Pierce, you here?"

"Out here. asshole."

I walk out to a screened room off the back of the house, where Pierce is drinking beer and looking at his laptop.

"Any updates on the Xander guy?" I ask as I take a beer from the makeshift cooler he has sitting next to him on the ground.

"I found some stuff, but nothing we didn't already know. He's an only child, his parents moved to Florida after he graduated from high school. They signed the house in Manteo over to him years ago, but as we all know he currently resides with one Emily Renee Fallon and he works in IT. He owns a small consulting business where he takes on a few jobs a year and those are enough to pay the bills, from what I can tell. He doesn't have any offshore accounts or excessive funds that I've found. Looks like he was on the radar from something when he was still a minor but the records are sealed so I can't get into them."

"Maybe he has a dark side and we can use that to our advantage? Did he leave the house today?"

"Nah, I drove by once and ran by another time and both times he was in the garage with it open working on that Bronco that the girl usually drives."

"Keep looking because I feel like there's something we can use you just haven't found it yet."

"Well now it's your turn, Dickhead, I have a shift to start with the girl. I ordered some pizza from that place up the way, there's leftovers in the fridge, help yourself."

"Also, the boss sent me some trackers, I put one on the guy's car. Grab the one on the counter on your way out. Maybe you will have a chance to place the other one," I tell him as I airdrop him the app for the trackers.

Pierce heads inside to grab his bag and prepare for a night of surveillance. I continue to drink my beer and think about our next move. I run inside to try and catch him. "Hey, we need to separate them. What if I try to get the girl alone."

"Abbott said collect intel, man."

"What better intel than getting her alone and asking a few questions?"

"Whatever, man, I gotta go."

"No seriously, tomorrow before you head back home, I want you to call me and tell me what route she takes for her run. Let's see if there is some sort of pattern with it.

From there we can figure out a way to put some pressure on her."

"I don't like this; I think we need to run it by Abbott, first."

"Quit being a bitch, Pierce, and do what I'm asking you to do."

Pierce grabs the remainder of his stuff, throws it aggressively into his bag, and heads out the door, slamming it behind him. I know he will come around. He didn't ask to be put on this assignment with me, hell I didn't ask to be put on this babysitting assignment but when Abbott told us about future opportunities and earning potential with deployments to Ecuador, I was all in. Looks like I need to keep reminding Pierce of that, though.

Then seeing her for the first time, all I want to do is mold her into a masterpiece I've envisioned. She's an enigma waiting to be solved. I'm the only one that truly understands her.

I go into my room to place the cup next to her hair tie. The hairs tickle my nose as I trace it along my face, breathing in her scent. Thoughts of her consume me and a feel another small twitch below my beltline. I need to talk to her and profess these feelings I have and that I only want to help her, now.

We were assigned this mission as a test. A test to make sure we can assimilate to the area and get our targets. She is more than a target now, though. I would do anything to have her.

XANDER

Walking back into the house I make a mental note to check and see what's up with Katniss, but first back to the office to finish setting up all of the security cameras. Looking at both of the monitors, I can see all of the cameras inside and outside the house are working fine. Everything is running in real time and is uploading correctly to the cloud with a seven-day history for now but we can adjust that as needed. Nobody is getting into this house or even near it like they did with Maverick last year but if they do, we will have it sent off-site for safety. I hear my phone ping from the other room, I ignore it for now, so I can finish this setup.

I head outside to move a few of the cameras that are off slightly causing a bit of a blind spot if they aren't moved, I grab my phone on the way out so I can make sure I get them where I need them without having to run back inside. Remembering the ping from earlier, I glance down seeing that it was an email that can wait until later. Once I'm satisfied with the camera positions, I head back inside to grab some lunch and figure out where to start with Katniss.

"I'm going to need you to be nice to me and tell me what's going on, because Ems will kill me if I do something that messes you up okay, ma'am." Great I'm officially going crazy. I'm talking to a hunk of metal.

I grab the keys and back the vehicle out of the garage just enough that I can move easily around it and work comfortably. I keep the vehicle on for a bit to see if I hear anything unusual or any noises that seem off. Everything sounds fine so far, but I'm not a mechanic. Turning the car off, I pop the hood and start to inspect everything.

After a few hours, I've found nothing wrong but went ahead and changed the oil, filter, spark plugs and basically gave her a tune-up so Ems wouldn't have to. I complained when I was a kid when my dad showed me how to do all of this stuff. Who knew that it would come in handy all these years later. Feeling a bit defeated by a car, I head inside to get cleaned up. I hear my phone ping again while in the shower reminding me of the email from earlier that I still need to check.

Em should be home in a bit and I still have to pack up a few more things of her dads and put them in the attic for now. The look on her face earlier, seeing the realization that these items were no longer taking up room in this part of the house, was sad but also, I feel like it's something she's been needing and wanting to do. After the last few items are stored away, I finally sit down to review the emails from earlier.

*X*ander- **I trust that you have told no one about the note I left you. I wanted to see if you would be willing to meet with me. I'm a friend of Mike Fallon's** and I'm in town for a short while. Would you consider grabbing lunch? He gave me something to hold onto in case something happened to him. Part of it you uncovered last year about Abbott. I think we can help each other here.

I hope to hear from you soon.
- Keith

*H*ow the hell did this person get my email? I think to myself. I've never heard Ems or Maverick mention a Keith in all of these years and I don't recall ever meeting someone named Keith when we were growing up. Who the hell is doing this? My first thoughts go to Abbott and his new set of goons that he likely has working for him. Before going down that slippery slope, I look at the email a bit closer and review the Metadata. When the information comes into view, I quickly push away from my desk and look around the room. What the fuck? It says the email came from the Wi-Fi that's located inside the house. How is that possible? I've been the only one here all day. I run into the office area with the security monitors and review the screens with all the real-time images. Nothing stands out. Looking closer at the feed, I rewind it to check and see if any cars on the street have come and gone in the past few hours, making sure to go back to the time that the original email was received. Again, nothing unusual. Opening the second email to see if it's somehow related to the first, I notice immediately that it is from this Keith person again.

*X*ander- You are probably wondering how I got your email or why it says it sent from inside the Fallon residence? You are not the only one that's good with computers. Please allow me to explain. Agree to meet with me but also know that you can't tell anyone, not even Emily. You will understand once we talk. This will be the last of the messages you receive from me. Emily's future depends on us meeting.

**Tomorrow Nags Head Pier at Noon and don't be late.
Keith**

If this person wanted to hurt me, he would have done it right? Why go through all of this to get my attention and ask to meet. This house isn't exactly Fort Knox and I'm not military trained, making me an easier target compared to my fiancée. Thinking through my options, I decide to meet with Keith tomorrow at Nags Head Pier. Ems will be at work and so far, there isn't really anything to tell her yet, so I'm not lying about anything because I don't know anything. I delete the messages from my email and head into the kitchen to start dinner because it's getting close to the time Ems usually gets home from work. Quickly, I throw together some burgers and make a small pasta salad for us. As I'm heading back in from starting the grill, my beautiful girl walks in from the garage.

"Hey handsome," she says before reaching up to greet me with a kiss.

"I have the grill going but we could always put dinner off for a bit if you have other things on your mind," I say while planting kisses along her jawline and down her neck.

"You are very persuasive, sir."

I run out to the grill to turn it off and run back in grabbing her hand to pull her up to our room.

We emerge almost an hour later hungrier than ever. "Now I really need some food," I tell her.

"I'll grab some wine if you want to start the grill back up; I won't distract you this time."

"Ems, you are the best kind of distraction though."

She winks at me as I head out to the patio to start everything up again. Ems joins me, hands me my wine, and we talk briefly about her day.

"Before I forget, I took a look at Katniss. Yes, I know from the look on your face, you prefer to handle any maintenance with her, but I was trying to take something off your plate. I started her up and she sounds fine, but I did go ahead and change the oil, filter, and plugs for you."

"You didn't have to do that but thank you. I planned to look at her this weekend but if she sounds fine and you went through and changed all those items, I'll probably go ahead and drive her tomorrow. Thanks for letting me borrow your car today, though."

"Ems, you can have whatever you want whenever you want."

"Well, that sounds like something I am definitely going to have you make good on at some point," she says as she laughs.

"Did you happen to see Abbott today while you were at the station?"

"No. I was near his office today and all the lights were on but he wasn't in there."

"Why were you by his office?"

"I was over there looking for something else that had to do with the ship he came off of. An engineering issue."

"I still don't like how your paths will cross from time to time but I trust that you and Mav know what you all are doing."

She leans her head on my chest. I'm sure it's to comfort

me more than her but I accept it and wrap my arm around her to squeeze her closer to me before going in to grab the burgers to throw on the grill.

We sit down to dinner and I tell her that all of the security cameras are properly placed. I send her the information for the app so she can also monitor from her phone as needed. The past few months I've shown her a few things here and there about what I do. I haven't gotten into specifics but just enough so she can work her way through some basic IT things. For instance, she could have figured out the email I received earlier also came from inside the house from our Wi-Fi. She knows how to review Metadata from different platforms and images and yet I decide to listen to the email that was sent earlier and choose not to tell her about it. Meeting with this person first makes more sense to see if it's even worth our time.

Em starts to clear our plates and clean up the kitchen while I make sure the grill is shut down for the night. I walk back in and see her admiring her engagement ring, the one that was her mothers.

"You were right, ya know."

"Probably, but about what this time?" she replies while smirking.

"Your mom knew that we would be together, it was only a matter of time."

"I love that she knew that. I wish they were here to see it."

"I know, babe." Pulling her to me, I hug her tightly.

"Tomorrow morning how about we run up to the beach? Like we did the other morning only this time, we also run back. Maybe I'll even let you drive Katniss."

"It's on!"

ABBOTT

*P*resent Day

The last trip to see my family was last year 2018, right before I was deployed to sea for a much larger assignment. Miguel is now almost ten as I look at his photo that sits on my desk in my home office. The photo is of him in his new baseball uniform for the youth league Maria signed him up for. My cold heart speeds up a bit at the sight of him.

After hanging up with that little pencil dick, Spencer, I can feel my blood pressure rising but Miguel's photo helps to regulate it. Stanley thinks these two are going to be helpful in shutting up the Fallons for good? They are liable to get us all killed from not thinking things through. Hopefully the package I sent was opened, so he knows I wasn't bluffing about them being watched.

I check the app on my phone and can see that one of the trackers has been activated. Spencer has something planned but what that is, I'm not quite sure.

Stanley says we have a new mission coming up in the next few weeks. A member from the Cartel will be here handling some business and wants to start using us to help launder money and pass drugs. Stanley says the guy is comparable to a ticking time bomb. He's known to shoot first, ask questions later. It's in my best interest to work quickly and have everything ready as soon as possible. So much for a break after deployment, tomorrow I get to snoop around and try to find some businesses that can be acquired for such a task. I like it better when I give the orders.

In my modest, dimly lit office I login to my personal PC and try to find businesses that are up for sale. A few catch my eye that are in Norfolk, VA. While that might be risky with the station there, with so many visitors to that base on a yearly basis, it makes the most sense. There's a restaurant wanting to sell, a laundromat looking to sell, and a bar. All could be decent cash flow businesses. That's what you need, right? Cash to clean the money. I make note of these businesses to discuss with Stanley.

After reviewing a few of the listings, I login to my bank account to transfer the monthly amount to Maria's account. I also add her as my beneficiary to transfer all funds upon death to her account. Some might see that as morbid; I see it as a contingency plan if I die.

I've dreamed of moving my family here. My heart aches knowing I can't. If I'm alive, they are safer in Ecuador. This is my penance. I clench my fists, feeling the weight of my decision. It's not that simple. The safety issues aren't much different from Ecuador. This choice keeps them safe. I've accepted that the only way out of this organization is to be killed when you know as much as I do. I've never been afraid to die because it will put me out of my misery, and I can go peacefully knowing my secrets will die with me when that time comes.

EMILY

Waking up to run to the beach requires a bit of an earlier start for the both of us as the annoying alarm starts to sound at 5:00 a.m.

"You still want to do this?"

Xander throws off the covers and jumps up to get dressed like a kid on the first day of school. "You said I could drive today. I'm not missing this for anything."

Xander is dressed and ready to go with keys in hand in record time. He is like a giddy teenager that just passed his driving test as he climbs into the driver's seat.

"You good, babe?"

"I usually don't care about cars, but I've been wanting to drive Katniss from the minute I saw David drive her around the neighborhood when we were younger."

"Well, start her up then."

He starts her up and heads to the lot near the bagel shop to park before we start our run. The illuminating grin on his face makes this moment so worth it. I can't help but smile at the pure joy he has on his face right now.

We get parked and take off for our run.

***

"Did you notice how many people were out today, Ems?"

"There were more than usual for sure. I noticed more yesterday as well. I don't know if it's tourists flocking here earlier and earlier each year or if they are new neighbors."

"What was with that one guy that we passed a few times? The blond one that kept checking you out. I saw him yesterday, when we ran our other route. Pretty sure he's Navy from the nautical star tattoo he had on his arm."

"Who was checking who out, Xander? I didn't see anyone specifically."

"How did you miss him, Ems? He gave off a creepy vibe almost like an Asher 2.0 persona."

"Now you are being ridiculous. I have to shower and get ready for work, but we can resume this later if you feel it's required." I give him my best *I really don't have time for this* look as I head off to get ready for work.

***

"Hey, about earlier, maybe it was nothing, but I would feel better today if you were more aware of your surroundings while at work, okay? We don't know who's working for Abbott yet and for all we know they are hiding in plain sight. Yes, I know you can take care of yourself, just tell me you will take extra precautions to make me feel better, okay?"

I wrap my arms around Xander's waist and tuck my head under his chin where I swear our bodies fit perfectly together then tell him, "I promise to be careful today and stay alert."

"Thank you, that's all I'm asking for. I'll see you tonight, Ems." He kisses my forehead.

I leave from the garage and off to the station. Xander's comment about not knowing who's working for Abbott now sticks with me. He's right, they could be in plain sight. As I'm leaving our neighborhood, I take notice of a pickup truck I pass on my way. It doesn't belong to any of our neighbors. It's been in this spot the past few days. The driver seems to be casually waiting on something or someone. I make a mental note of the vehicle, the driver, and the plate to see if anyone else has noticed it around lately then continue my trip to the station.

* * *

I get to the station at my scheduled time, and I'm confronted with a bunch of files from the last ship that returned to port.

Amongst them are a few system maintenance requests and daily reports. I run through the reports first and then swing over to Ander's office to grab him to help with the maintenance requests. Hoping to knock them out quickly.

"Anders, do you have some free time today to help me with some system updates on the last ship that came in?"

"Sure thing. Let me finish this last report and we can head down there."

"Sounds good, I'll wait outside your office."

Anders office is close to Abbott's office, so I take a few large steps in his direction and notice his door is open. I can hear his voice echo from inside the room.

"I put an offer in on one but the other two were above the original asking price, so I let those go. I think we are in a good spot based on what the Realtor told me."

I quickstep back to Ander's office just as he walks out.

"Ready to go?"

"Waiting on you, Anders."

"Kiss my ass, Fallon."

"Not even with somebody else's lips, Anders."

He lets out a deep belly laugh and rolls his eyes as we head to the ship.

The maintenance repairs and service updates take much longer than I thought they would. We try to get through them quickly, but as soon as we finish one thing another item requires an update. This goes on for hours. I text Xander to let him know not to hold dinner for me as I finally get to my car around 6:00 p.m. making it so I won't be home until close to 7:30 p.m.

XANDER

*A*fter Ems leaves for the day, I spend a few hours cleaning up the house then quickly get cleaned up. I hurry around the house grabbing my work items such as my laptop, phone, and so on. I head out the door and drive to the pier.

Looking at my watch, I see that Keith is now late. Not that I know what he looks like, but I've arrived fifteen minutes before the requested time at Nags Head Pier and nobody is here. Well, nobody that looks like they are meeting anyone in particular. I walk over to the restaurant that's a part of the pier. The bar on the other hand is packed with only one open seat. Making myself comfortable, I order a beer while I wait.

The gentleman next to me gets up to leave and slightly bumps me as he exits the stool. I turn for the niceties that usually follow after someone bumps you, but he's already gone. When I turn back, there's a note on the bar next to my beer.

Meet me on the beach after your beer.

Who is this guy? I think to myself. I finish my beer

quickly and head out toward the beach. Even in April, the beach has a fair amount of people. I see one person near the water who could blend in if needed but also doesn't exactly belong. He was wearing the same thing as the gentleman that bumped into me at the bar, khaki cargo paints and a floppy hat. I walk toward the water but keep about three feet from him in case this isn't Keith.

"Xander, thank you for meeting me."

"Keith, I presume? You want to explain to me what this is all about now?"

"Not here. You will receive a text in a few minutes with an address. You will drive to that location without telling anyone about this or any future meetings. Everything will be explained to you shortly."

"And if I don't show up?"

"We have your nuts in a vice, open your phone, Xander."

I open my phone to a new message and a picture of Asher's very dead body staring back at me. My stomach rolls at the sight of it. Knowing I'm defeated I nod my head in agreement.

"See you in a few minutes, Xander."

I watch Keith as he maneuvers through the people on the beach and up through the crowd on the pier. He disappears before my eyes as he blends in with the crowd.

* * *

Heading back to my car, I feel my phone vibrate from an incoming message. Retrieving it from my pocket, I see an address as promised. Once inside my car, I open my GPS app and enter the address to guide me to the location. It takes me a little over five minutes to get to an old restaurant that's been closed for a few years. Last I heard, the owners had a falling out and decided to close their doors. Now the building sits vacant and has been up for sale ever since. Today the for-sale sign now has a sold sign over it. I pull into the empty lot and check the address to make sure it's the correct one that was sent to me. After confirming that it is I head to the front of the building and walk inside the door that is slightly ajar.

"Hello?"

"Head back to the kitchen, toward the back of the restaurant, Xander."

The voice sounds like Keith's from earlier, so I do as he requests. Once in the kitchen, I look around. There are three men. Two of them are dressed in all black, Keith is in the middle of them. There are four chairs in a circle in the middle of the room and outlines along the wall where appliances once were. The rest of the room is empty.

"Have a seat, Xander."

Looking around the room and again at the three men, I decide to take a seat.

"What is this all about? Who are you with?"

"I told you I'm an old friend of Mike Fallon. Well, more of an acquaintance really. I knew him years ago. He reached out right before his last mission with some interesting information that had been brought to his attention. He gave me a few paper files to review until he got back. He wasn't certain and said he would have proof after his next deployment. As you know, he didn't return from that deployment. Since then, I've been working on gathering intel on my own to bring to my boss, but it's been a slow process and frankly, I had almost given up until Maverick triggered an alert last year."

"So, you work with Abbott, fucking great. Well, I don't know anything, so you are wasting your time."

"The exact opposite there, tiger, we are wanting to take Abbott down and Stanley."

"Why did you reach out to me?"

"Because there has been some chatter with Abbott's crew that they have been watching you. You have something they want."

"What's that?"

"You."

"Me? Why me?"

"They know what you can do. That you are really good with computers, and they would like to borrow your skillset to assist them with a future endeavor."

"And if I don't help them?"

"You've seen what they are capable of, they will go after your family and threaten them or worse until you agree to help them."

"Where do you come into all of this?"

"We want to help you get in with them. What would you do to protect Emily?"

"I would do anything."

"Anything?"

"I would do absolutely anything for her. I would die for her."

"Would you kill for her if you had to?"

"If it were to save her or her family absolutely. She's everything to me."

"Okay, that's what we needed to hear. We will get you in with Abbott. Once you are in, and they give you access to their computer system, you will plant a script that allows the room to be recorded and relayed back to us. It's one-way, so you won't hear anything from us, but we can hear you. If you feel compromised or things turn south, you can say a safe word and we will be in there within seconds."

"What's the safe word?"

"Pineapple."

"How in the fuck am I going to use that casually in a sentence?"

Keith looks at each of the men in the room before leaning down to become eye level with me.

"Xander, if your life is at risk, I really don't think you will be caring about the use of the word."

"Fair point." I take a few minutes to consider what he's telling me before asking, "What's this future endeavor?"

"The chatter is that they have a Cartel friend coming to the states from Ecuador to set up a laundering operation near Norfolk, VA. Abbott has been spotted checking out a few places near the station that are currently up for sale. One of them is a restaurant, almost exactly laid out like this one. We had some competitive bids put on the other two places; a bar and a laundromat to push them to the restaurant. Assuming that works, they will be setting up their drug smuggling/money laundering operation through the restaurant."

"Where do I come into this? I don't know anything about running a restaurant, smuggling drugs, or washing money."

"They will need someone to set up the offshore accounts for the Cartel. To have a way for the funds to funnel to said accounts. That's where you come in."

"They won't let me live once those are set up. Have you all not seen Ozark? I'm a loose end!"

"We will be with you the whole time. You won't be able to see us, but we will be there. Remember the safe word."

"Oh, right, pineapple. Fuck your pineapple, Keith."

I get up to leave but the other guys in the room block my path. Annoyed at my predicament, I turn to face Keith. The look on my face is that of a petulant child who doesn't want to do what's being asked of them. There is no other choice and I know that as Keith tries to remind me.

"Xander, you said you would do anything for Emily. She will go to prison. Asher's body was discovered, and we have her location via satellite with him last. A witness clocked her at a bar with him the same weekend. It doesn't look good for her, Xander. Her prints were also pulled from his body. You do this, I will wipe the slate completely clean for her."

"How do I know you have that authority? Who the fuck are you, man?"

"I work for the DEA; we have been tracking this operation for over ten years. This goes higher than you or I know, but Abbott and Stanley are the main runners. You help us get them, I wipe the slate clean for Emily and she can live happily ever after with you. You walk out that door, she spends her remaining days in a supermax prison. Oh, and, Xander, this part is important; you can't tell anyone anything about this operation or what you will be doing. The only way this all works is if nobody else knows about it. Including your girl. Now I need an answer."

EMILY

I walk into the house and Xander is there with a glass of wine in hand. He is too good to me.

"While I want to drink this more than you know, I really want to change and go for a run to clear my head. It's been a day. I was stuck on a ship doing maintenance requests and system updates almost all day. I really don't miss that being my life for months at a time."

"Let me put this in the fridge, I will go change, and go with you."

"Babe, you don't have to go with me, I'm not going to be long. I'm not doing my usual route, just a quick two miles. Twenty minutes tops, then a quick shower followed by the wine you poured, and then we can catch up about our days."

"Okay, I'll warm up some food for us while you are gone."

"I don't deserve you at all, Xander."

I kiss him quickly and dart up to change into running clothes and out the front door.

I run around a few of the blocks near our house and

down near the sound. There's a short path that cuts through to the canal that's always covered in pine needles from the trees that surround the area. Around the canal is a trail that loops around and leads back to the parking lot, or you can continue on to another neighborhood. As I near the lot, I'm about half a mile from the house as someone calls my name from behind me.

"Emily."

I turn around and see a person that fits the description of who Xander described earlier from our run, down to the nautical tattoo on his arm.

"Do I know you?"

"I know your family. I've been trying to get you alone to talk to you. We have so many things in common."

That doesn't sound fucking creepy at all, I think to myself before making an excuse to leave. "I'm running late for something." I start to turn to head back home and he jogs in front of my path. I shift to the side to try and go around.

"Give me a few minutes to explain."

My stomach sours as a bad feeling starts to build inside. "I really have to go. Maybe I'll see you around."

He grabs my wrist with an iron grip like hold and forces me to turn into him. He is taller than me and outweighs me by at least ninety pounds. I'm going to need more than a few quick moves to get out of this.

"Hey, buddy, how about you let me go and we can have that talk. I can delay my plans a few minutes." I put my free hand on his chest and bat my eyelashes hoping to sell this.

"That's all I'm asking, Emily."

He frees my wrist and moves my hair behind my ear. I let my face follow as if his touch means something to me.

"I've been watching you for some time and had wanted to talk to you before now, but you are never alone. I got the gifts that you've been leaving for me."

He reaches into a pocket and pulls out a broken rubber band.

"This one is my favorite. It still smells like you."

He inhales deeply as he holds the rubber band to his face. Who the fuck is this guy? With that, I know I need to get out of here and put as much distance between us as I can. He steps toward me trying to close the small gap between us. I scan my surroundings to see what I can use as a weapon. There's a decent size rock past him and a large stick to the right of him. If I can distract him, and get to one of them, I can get out of this. Luring him in close enough to strike should allow me time to move toward a potential weapon.

"Did you find all of the items? I left you several."

He places his hands on my hips and brings his forehead to mine. "You left me the hair tie and the coffee cup."

"You didn't get my shirt? I left you my running shirt near the house." He smiles with pure joy and lets out an audible gasp. I use his moment of gross elation to put my plan into motion as his hands lessen their hold.

I place my hands on his shoulders preparing to strike. I bring my knee up between his legs with incredible force. He doubles over and I take that moment to sprint past him toward the rock. The mightier of my two weapon choices. He recovers quickly and lunges for me from behind bracing my arms at my sides. My face hits a bed of pine needles before my hands have a chance to break free to avoid impact. He flips me over. Immediately I can see that he is pissed.

"I finally get you alone and this is how you treat me?" he says as he tries to straddle me. "This fire inside me keeps burning for you. I needed to see you, to feel you. I know you feel it too."

"Get the fuck off me, you psycho."

I try to push him off me but he has my legs braced tightly with his. The sheer weight of him makes it difficult to move.

He rips my shirt in an upward motion trying to remove it but instead tears it. "No one else deserves you. We are destined to be together, no matter what the cost. I know last year you thought you were so smart after the shit you pulled. You still need to be punished for that but first, let me show you how a real man feels. A man who would sacrifice everything to be with you, Emily. The other day when you smiled at me, I knew it was time we met in person."

His eyes are so dark and vacant. He talks like he's in love with me, but I think maybe he plans to kill me. I can see that in his cold dead eyes. He's clearly delusional if he thinks I would reciprocate any of these feelings. I need to fight and get myself far enough away from him before he tries to finish what he's started.

When he shifts his weight slightly, I'm able to free one of my legs. I swiftly move my knee into the air making contact with my attacker. He falls backward almost completely off of me. Pushing myself up and using my feet to push away from the person, I start feeling around on the ground for any object I can use as a weapon. My hand grabs onto a cold rock that I located earlier. He pulls my legs back towards him, I swing my weapon and clock him in the mouth with a jagged stone. A few teeth are knocked out and blood is dripping from his mouth. Quickly, I jump up and round-kick him in the head rendering him unconscious.

I grab my phone and call Uncle Paul and tell him to bring the car and not to tell Xander until we get to his house. Xander will kill him on-site.

Uncle Paul arrives in less than a minute and helps me

slide the attacker into the backseat. We call Xander and have him meet us at his house. My uncle looks at me briefly and makes another call.

"I need medical assistance, please. One person, send the woman please."

"I'm fine uncle, he caught me off guard. It looks worse than it is." Grabbing his free hand, I try to convey that I'm fine but he ignores my attempt.

"You are getting evaluated. No arguments."

Xander is in front of the garage as we pull into the driveway. He moves slightly to allow the car into the garage and sees someone lying in the backseat who is bleeding and directs his look back to me.

"Xander, help me with this guy."

Xander comes over to me and sees my torn shirt and marks on my face and hands. He's careful as he barely touches me. Reaching for his hands, I hold them in mine trying to give him reassurance that I'm fine. He's laser-focused on the guy in the backseat.

"What the hell happened? Your watch sent me an alert that your heart rate had spiked. When I checked your location, it was the trail behind our house. I got in the car to find you but Uncle Paul called before I left."

"I will tell you once we get him inside and restrained. Please, help my uncle first."

Xander grabs the guy under the arms and tugs him abruptly from the vehicle. The guy lets out a moan as he starts to stir. Xander drops him to the garage floor and straddles over him punching him hard in the face multiple times.

His blue eyes turn a deep dark blue and for a moment I almost don't recognize the look on his face.

"Xander, what are you doing?"

"I don't know what happened yet but I'm guessing this

guy attacked you and you did this to him. I wasn't there so I'm getting my turn in now. Wait, this is the guy from this morning, Ems? I told you!"

Xander picks the guy back up under his arms and Uncle Paul has his legs as they move up the stairs and into the house. Xander is not taking any extra care to avoid obstacles and manages to hit his head on anything that will sit still.

They sit him in a chair as Paul leaves the room and comes back with zip-ties to use as restraints. There's a soft knock at the back door.

"Emily, will you let her in please?"

I leave the room to see who it is, when I'm greeted by the nurse from last year. She looks exactly the same; scrubs, hair pulled back, and no makeup on.

"Emily, we need to stop meeting like this. May I come in?"

"Yes, Ma'am."

We both walk to where everyone else is in the living room and Uncle Paul tells us to use the spare bedroom. Xander follows us but the nurse stops him at the door.

"It's alright I want him to come in."

He walks into the room and sits on the bed next to me. He's looking me over and I must look frightful because the look on his face is almost that of a scared child. I reach for his hand and squeeze it to let him know I'm fine.

"Take your time, Emily, but when you are ready, I would like you to tell me what happened."

"I got home from work and decided I wanted to go for a run to clear my head. There's a quick two-mile route near the house and I was already on my way back. I had maybe a half mile left when I heard my name. I turned around and that guy tried to strike up a conversation. When I went to leave, he blocked my path. In that moment,

I realized I needed to outsmart him. I pretended to listen and play along with his visions of us as I took in the area to look for a weapon and a way out. When I got him to let down his guard a little, I took the opportunity to rack him and move toward one of the two weapons I tracked. He tackled me, flipped me over, and started talking to me like he knew me and was infatuated with me. A part of him seems to think I felt the same way. I knew what his intentions were as he tried to rip off my shirt and told me he was going to show me what a real man felt like."

Xander clenches his fits and begins to stand but I pull him back down to sit on the bed before continuing on, "When he shifted his weight, I kneed him and found something to use as a weapon. That allowed me a quick minute to get up but because he was still alert, I didn't trust that he wouldn't chase me so I incapacitated him with a round kick to the head. Once I was sure he was out, I phoned Uncle Paul because I knew Xander here would have killed him."

"Thank you for going through that with me, Emily. The cuts on your hand are from wielding the rock then I assume and likely the contact with that and his face?"

"Yes."

"The scratches are from him trying to grab you?"

"Yes. Him pulling me back toward him."

"What about the marks and bruising to your face?"

"That was from him tackling me, he never hit me in the face. He had my arms tight against me when we fell. I couldn't stop my face from hitting the ground."

"Is there anything else you need or want to tell me."

"No, that was everything that happened. I'm glad it was me that he attacked and not someone else that didn't know how to defend themselves."

"This wasn't a coincidence, Ems. You weren't a target of

convenience. That's the guy I kept seeing on our routes. You need to tell your family that we saw him again this morning. I think he might be working with Abbott or hell let me question him."

Xander gets up to leave the room, but I quickly block the door.

"Hey, my uncle will handle this alright. You are upset and I completely understand why. Let him question him and see what he can find out. I know you want to help but the tactics that might be needed, I don't think you have the stomach for."

"I do right now." But, he nods in agreement, and I turn back to the nurse to see what else is needed. She cleans up my cuts before acknowledging that it's fine to leave. We all head out to the living room where my attacker is still being held and Uncle Paul is now sitting across from him.

The nurse keeps walking until she is out the back door and off into the night.

The mystery man comes to and spits out the blood that had pooled in his mouth either from my kick or Xander's punches.

"Who sent you?" asks Uncle Paul.

"They will never stop coming for you. There will always be someone to replace me. I've been trying to get to Emily. To protect her, get her out of here. We are meant to be together. You can't save her from them. None of you can."

Uncle Paul ignores the fictional statements coming from this guy's mouth. I have to keep my hand in Xander's to make sure he doesn't charge at the guy and rip his head off.

"Who do you work for?"

"You already know the answer to that."

"Abbott?"

"He's our handler, yes, but he isn't the boss."

"Stanley?"

"You aren't as slow as you look, old man."

Xander takes a step forward toward the battered captive, but Uncle Paul raises a hand for him to stop.

"What is it that you are after?"

"They want the intel from the safes and the files from Operation Cobalt that were on the drive that her idiot brother downloaded last year. I could have protected you, Emily. Why can't you see that? I did all of this for you. For us."

Who is this guy?

"What if I told you we destroyed all of that intel," says Uncle Paul.

"You didn't."

"What makes you say that?"

"Someone made copies of the file that ties Stanley to drug runs in Ecuador. That same someone downloaded information that links Abbott to David and Mike Fallon's murders. Who do you think gave him the order?"

"Stan..."

As Uncle Paul started to reply "Stanley" the glass in the front bay window shatters. We instinctively all duck for cover. No other shots are heard. As we begin to stand, I notice our captive is slumped in his chair. We all notice quickly that a bullet hit him center mass. I check for a pulse but there isn't one.

Uncle Paul checks the man's clothing and I hand a phone over to Xander that I found in his pocket.

After a few minutes, Uncle Paul locates a very small device that could be a microphone or camera. He takes it over to his counter and destroys it with a meat tenderizer.

"Who was that guy?"

"I don't know but this morning when I left, I remembered your comment about us being watched and noticed a truck down the street from our house. The driver in it looked very laidback, like he was waiting on someone or something but also like he didn't belong."

"Have you seen that vehicle before, Emily?"

"A few times but today was the first time I recall seeing someone in it. Black pickup, regular tires, and rims are not like some of the lifted ones you see around here. I think it was a Dodge Ram and the license plate was from Norfolk, VA."

"Is it just me that thinks we should leave after that guy got shot?"

"He was an asset that went rogue, Xander, they weren't here for us this time. He said too much so they took him out. As he said, they will keep sending people like him. It was probably another one of him that took him out."

"So, what's the plan?"

"We call Maverick and Mel and let them know that we are being watched. We need to make sure all of our intel is someplace safe. I say we move up our family dinner to tomorrow. We will have it at your place, Emily, thanks to Xander having all of the security cameras installed, it's as safe as any right now."

"What do we do with this guy?" asks Xander as he points to the dead guy.

"I'll make a call."

ABBOTT

My phone rings and I see the number. It's one of the two idiots we hired to keep tabs on the Fallons.

"What?"

"It's Pierce. We have a situation. Spencer is off the rails and he's gone rogue. He just attacked the girl and with a quick turn of events he's now being held hostage at the uncle's place."

My thoughts start to race and a cold shiver runs down my spine.

"And? Did he hurt the girl? Do you think he's going to talk or something or does he have our plans written down and on his person for them to find?"

"She seems fine. And while he is stupid, he isn't that stupid to have them written down, but he is that cocky enough to talk to them."

"After he got home the other day, he started talking about doing recon on the boyfriend and trying to get her alone. I took the time to place a small microphone on his running jacket a few days ago. He wears that thing all the time or has it in his vehicle with him. He's currently wearing it and I can hear him starting to stir."

Tension hangs in the air. The mission's success hangs in the balance. I know we need to neutralize Spencer before he divulges anything specific.

"Put your phone on speaker I want to hear what they ask him."

"Yes, sir."

"Who sent you?"

That's Paul's voice, I would recognize it anywhere, I think to myself.

"They will never stop coming for you. There will always be someone to replace me. I've been trying to get to Emily. To protect her, get her out of here. We are meant to be together. You can't save her from them. None of you can."

"Who do you work for?"

"You already know the answer to that."

"Abbott?"

Pierce cuts into the conversation to tell me, "Sir if this goes sideways, I can take him out. I have a clear shot. No other casualties."

A knot tightens in my stomach. It's one thing to take out the enemy but one of our own has a different feel to it.

"Let's wait and see what he does first," I tell Pierce as the conversation continues.

"He's our handler yes but he isn't the boss."

"Stanley?"

"You aren't as slow as you look, old man."

"What is it that you are after?"

"They want the intel from the safes and the files from Operation Cobalt that were on the drive that her idiot brother downloaded last year. I could have protected you,

Emily. Why can't you see that? I did all of this for you. For us."

"What if I told you we destroyed all of that intel," says Paul.

"You didn't."

"What makes you say that?"

"Someone made copies of the file that ties Stanley to drug runs in Ecuador. That same someone downloaded information that links Abbott to David and Mike Fallon's murders. Who do you think gave him the order?"

Sometimes the decisions are black and white and sometimes they are not.

I've heard enough. "Pierce, take him out."

"Stan..."

I hear the shot fired and I end the call.

"FUCK! These incompetent assholes!" I scream into the room. I know I need to call Stanley to provide an update but I need to think about my next steps. This really only goes one way now.

After a few minutes of contemplating, I dial his number and wait for him to pick up. The task is daunting but needs to be handled. After a few rings, his voice comes on the line.

"You have an update?"

"One you don't want to hear."

"I'm waiting."

I let out a heavy sigh and then recount the events leading up to this call.

"Spencer went rogue and Pierce had to take him out. He attacked the girl and was captured by Paul. During questioning, he provided both of our names."

There's silence. I assume it's him processing the information I gave him.

"In what capacity did he provide our names?"

"He told them that I'm their handler and that you give the orders."

"Pierce took him out before he could continue with any specific details. But we've been compromised."

"You know what this means don't you?"

"I do."

"You have two options here, Abbott. You speed up the timeline and grab the kid to open the offshore accounts along with taking out the rest of the family or I make sure your little family in Ecuador disappears."

I don't say anything for a brief moment the silence is deafening. Did he say my family?

"Ahh, you didn't think that I knew about them, did you? You weren't that clever my friend. You can retrace your steps all you want but I still had you followed and my scouts told me that you developed a personal connection to a local in Ecuador. I kept sending you all of these years to confirm that and to gather additional intel on whether or not it was more than a simple fling. Maria and Miguel, is it? They appear happy even though they have ties to an international criminal."

"You won't fucking touch them, you bastard. They have nothing to do with this!"

"Then follow the order, grab the kid, and take out the Fallons like you were told. This is bigger than you know, Abbott, I'm not the only one calling the shots here. I told you before that I'm the rook but there are more powerful pieces in play, right now. You have put a target on both of our backs. Make your choice."

The heaviness settles over me. The price of leadership and the role I signed up for has a very harsh reality.

"Consider it made."

EMILY

A few men appear through the same door that the nurse left. Leaving them to do whatever it is they came to do, Xander and I go into the spare room to call Maverick.

"Mav, we need to move up the family dinner to tomorrow, our house."

"Everything okay?"

"We will talk about it when you all get here but no better time than the present to teach Mel and Evelyn about go bags."

"Understood. We will be there tomorrow after work."

"And Mav?"

"Yep?"

"Watch your ass."

"Do the same, Emme."

After hanging up with Mav, I tell Xander that they will be here after work.

"Why did you want Mav to talk to Mel about go bags?"

"Last time she was kidnapped. This time they have

Evelyn to worry about. It's safer for them to disappear and let us handle whatever our plan is."

"I was half expecting you to tell me to do the same, Ems. I was fully prepared to have our first real fight."

"Are you kidding, we need your expertise, Xander. Plus, I focus better when you are close by," I tell him as I wrap him in a hug and nuzzle his neck with my nose while planting a few kisses.

"I guess makeup sex will have to wait for another day then."

I smack his arm and we look down the hall to see if the coast is clear yet.

"The cleaners are gone. You can come out now you two."

Xander stops me before we are out of the room. "Cleaners? What is it that your uncle does now, Em?"

"I'm guessing it's better we don't know."

He grabs my hand to lead us back into the living room. You would never know someone had been shot in the middle of the room. Even the glass from the window has been cleaned up and two men are installing a new pane now.

"Uncle, I think you should stay with us tonight."

"Emily, I will be fine. This was a statement being made to tie up a punk imbecile whose ego got the best of him, nothing more."

"Okay, but if you change your mind, you know where we are."

We say our goodbyes, walk out into the night, and back down the street to our house. Xander grabs my hand and folds me into his side. I know he's worried and also probably beating himself up for not going with me. Once we are inside, I pull him over to the couch and sit down next to him.

"Xander, I'm fine."

"Em, I should have gone with you."

"Here is something that you don't want to hear. That guy was right. They won't stop coming for us until we end this. You can't be with me every minute of every day."

"The hell I can't!"

I crawl into his lap and let him hold me while I listen to his heartbeat. This is one fight I will lose with him. I've never had this kind of connection with anyone else. He feels like home.

At some point Xander must have carried me to bed, because my alarm is going off next to my head. I get changed into my workout clothes and at the bottom of the stairs, Xander is there waiting to join me. Keeping his word, he isn't letting me out of his sight.

We avoid the route from last night, more for him, and take another two-mile route in the opposite direction. Once we are back at the house, I get cleaned up quickly so we can have breakfast together before I have to leave.

"What's your day look like, babe?"

"I'm sure Anders and I have another stack of system updates for other ships that have come in the past few days. How about you? What exciting things are going on in the IT consulting world?"

"I'm finishing up one project for a client and have a new potential one in the works."

"Should I know or ask what it is that you do exactly?"

Xander brings me a plate of food around the counter, sets it down, and then turns my bar stool to face him as he grabs my face and leans his forehead on mine.

"If I tell you, I will have to kill you, Ems." He lets out this massive laugh. "I tried to be serious when I said that."

"So, that's a no then?"

"I don't know what you think it is that I do, babe, but

I'm just really good at computers. I basically build programs for different companies. It can be anything from increasing their database access on certain platforms to training modules for their IT department."

I look at him a bit leery and not sure if he's telling me the full truth but go back to eating my food regardless.

"We aren't done talking about this, but I'm hungry and I'm going to be late to work."

He laughs as we both finish our food and prepare for our day. The calm before the storm settles in because I know what's about to happen this evening when we all sit down to discuss our plans to confront Abbott head-on.

I'm almost to the garage when Xander pulls me by the waist into a tight hug.

"If you see Abbott today avoid him, please. We will figure this all out tonight but for the next ten or so hours promise me you will fix ships or systems, give Anders hell, and then drive home."

"I will do all of the above, especially give Anders hell."

He kisses my forehead and I leave for work. Once I hit the other side of the bridge leaving the Outer Banks, I phone Maverick. "Hey, I sent you a link that is tracking someone, will you open it and tell me where it's sitting?"

"Morning, Emme, I'm great, thanks for asking."

"I know. I'm sorry, I'm all business today but last night has my head spinning and yes, I will explain everything later."

"It's sitting at the station."

"Perfect, that's all I needed."

"What are you up to?"

"Nothing. I wanted to make sure that it wasn't near the house is all."

"Okay. We will see you tonight. And, Emme, don't go do anything I would do, got it?"

"Mav, there aren't many things left that you wouldn't do."

"Whatever, Emme, you know what I mean."

"That I do, Mav."

ABBOTT

*A*fter my phone call with Stanley, I contemplated my choices. Do I protect my family in Ecuador or end this once and for all? I think through the past several years and how different my life would have been had I not agreed to be Stanley's muscle. But I wouldn't have met Maria and she wouldn't have had Miggy. The decisions I made were my own and at the time they were what I thought was best. They were never meant to be part of this equation. I thought I was methodical with my planning. Played my cards close to my chest. But he's been a few steps ahead of me the whole time. I don't know how I missed it but that ends now.

I make my decision and call Pierce to fill him in, but on a need-to-know basis. His phone rings a few times before he answers.

"Pierce."

"I have a task for you. It supersedes everything else. This will move up our timeline pretty quickly."

"Of course, Sir. I'm ready to carry out any orders."

"I need you to grab the guy tomorrow. He holds the key to a phase in our operation. We need his expertise."

"Do you want me to break in to get him?"

"No, but if he leaves the house for anything, take him then."

"Sir, he doesn't leave the house that much."

"If he doesn't leave, get creative, Pierce."

"Understood, Sir. Consider it done, Sir."

"And Pierce?"

"Yes, Sir?"

"Don't fucking hurt him. We need him alive. For now, anyway."

"Yes, Sir. What do you want me to do with him once I have him?"

"I'll send you an address. It will be in Norfolk, VA, so make sure you secure him. We can't afford any mistakes."

"Got it. Any particular time you want him delivered by?"

"Tomorrow. The time is irrelevant. We need him to work for us for a bit in order to get items finalized before an out-of-town friend comes to visit."

"I won't let you down, Sir."

"See that you don't. I have someone else waiting for your spot if you can't make this happen. If you do make this happen, consider yourself promoted."

"Understood, Sir."

Hanging up with Pierce, I stare at my phone and debate about making this next call.

I scroll to the contact in my phone that I haven't even thought about in years. A decade of evading justice has finally taken its toll. The weight of my crimes is starting to feel unbearable. With a heavy sigh, I select the number. Who knows if it even belongs to him anymore? Will he remember the deal he made with me all those years ago? Is that deal still valid? So much time has passed, I'm sure they have other people that can work with them now.

Fuck! I hit the name and the phone starts to ring.

"Agent Morris."

"How about those Tigers?"

"Abbott?"

"It's been a long time."

"It has. I wasn't even sure you were still alive."

"Not sure how to take that comment so I'm going to let that slide. You ready to play ball?"

"I think it's time for me to cooperate."

"You remember where we met all those years ago?"

"I do," I reply.

"Meet me there in an hour. And Abbott?"

"What?"

"Once you start down this road, that's it. There's no going back."

"I'm aware. That's why it took me ten years to make this call. It's time to make amends. I'll give you everything you need to dismantle this operation and bring everyone down that's tied to it."

"Makes sense about you waiting so long to call me. See you in an hour."

I hang up my phone and fall into my desk chair. There's no turning back now. Powder keg is lit and it's about to blow. Time to end this once and for all.

EMILY

"Xander, everyone will be here in about ten minutes. How are the vegetables and chicken doing out on the grill?"

There's no response from him even though he's directly across from me in the kitchen. He has a vacant look on his handsome face.

"Xander? Babe?"

"What? Sorry, Ems, did you say something?"

"You, okay?

"I'm fine. Everything is fine. I'm tired is all. What were you saying? I'm listening now."

"I was checking to see where we were with the vegetables and chicken that are on the grill."

"Oh shit."

Xander sets down his wine glass and quickly moves to the back door.

"On it," he says as he hurries through the doorway and out to the patio.

He returns a few minutes later with our grilled items

and places them in the oven on warm until the rest of the family arrives.

Uncle Paul arrives first followed shortly by Mel, Mav, and Evelyn. We go through our quick greetings and catch up on Mel and Evelyn's day while we make our plates. Once everyone is seated, I begin.

"Thank you all for changing our dinner plans to tonight. I'll get right to it. Last night while I was on a run near here, someone tried to attack me."

Looking around the table, I can see that I have everyone's attention and continue on.

"He tackled me from behind and attempted to do more but I was able to fight him off and incapacitate him until Uncle Paul arrived."

Maverick clenches and unclenches his jaw waiting for me to continue.

"We took him back to the house where Uncle Paul questioned him. During that time someone took him out. Once we realized whoever it was that took him out was only after that guy, we searched him and found what we believe was a tracker and/or microphone of some sort. That has since been destroyed."

Maverick stops me to ask, "Emme, are you okay?"

"I'm fine, but I wanted us to meet because Abbott and whoever is working for him are at it again. I placed a tracker on Abbott's car the other day."

"The one you had me check on earlier?" asks Maverick.

"The same one, yes. From what I can tell, he personally isn't following us when I look at his location and time stamps within the app. The locations are consistent with his house in Kill Devil Hills, the station, and some restaurant near the station. Well, a place that was a restaurant that is."

"Why a restaurant or old restaurant?" Mel inquires.

"I'm not sure but I overheard a conversation the other day outside of Abbott's office. He was talking about real estate and putting in an offer on a restaurant."

Xander turns his head to look at me with confusion. I'm assuming it's because I'm supposed to be avoiding Abbott but I did tell him our paths may cross from time to time.

Someone's phone rings, I look around the table to see who it belongs to as Xander apologizes and then tells us he has to take it. He gets up from the table and leaves the room.

"Another thing I wanted to bring up is a black pickup truck, Dodge Ram I believe, has been near the house lately with a man in his late twenties sitting inside it. Anyone else notice this vehicle?"

Uncle Paul speaks up, "I noticed it yesterday, Emily. Shortly after you usually leave for work, I went to the hardware store to pick up an order. It was there when I left and also when I returned about twenty minutes later. If I were a betting man, I would bet he works for Abbott."

Xander walks back into the room looking a bit flustered as he runs his hands through his hair before joining us at the table.

"Everything okay, Xander?"

He grabs my hand and squeezes it as he tells me, "It was the jeweler letting us know that the rings are ready to be picked up. I can grab them on my way to Norfolk tomorrow."

"Norfolk? Why would you be heading to Norfolk?" I ask him.

"Remember when I told you I had a potential new client?"

"Yes."

"Well, they called when I hung up with the jeweler. They need me to create a program tomorrow for them. The good news is that I've done one very similar to this request so it won't take me long. I will probably even beat you back home."

My silence I'm sure portrays my dislike of this new information. Why does he have to be away from the house tomorrow? I won't admit this to him, but having all of the added security was peace of mind for me as well, when I'm so far away at work.

"The program has to be done tomorrow?" asks Uncle Paul.

"Unfortunately, yes. I know I don't have the family's military background, but I shouldn't be long. I'll have my phone on me the entire time. Would you all feel better if I shared my location?"

A resounding "YES" is heard from the family surrounding the dining room table.

Xander laughs, "Okay, I will share it with you all if that will help ease your concern."

I still don't like this, but I know it's his job and we can't keep living our lives in fear.

"While discussing protecting our loved ones, I talked to Mel about go bags. We have a plan in place for her and Evelyn. We will tell you that once the plan is in motion, she will not be reachable by anyone except me. She has a few different burner phones, cash and several ID's that Uncle Paul had made for her awhile back. The plan for them is to lay low. We have a five-day plan figured out for now that will keep them on the move. Mel, remember if anything comes through to one of the phones other than the phrase we discussed, keep moving."

"I understand and you all please keep yourselves safe. And Emily?"

"Yes, Mel?"

Mel covers Evelyn's ears and says, "End this shit."

"Yes sister, that's why we are here. To figure out how to do that."

XANDER

*T*en minutes earlier.

My phone starts to ring so I excuse myself from my dining room table.

"Hello?" I answer in a hushed voice.

"Tomorrow is when we need you to get caught."

"This isn't the best time right now to talk about this."

"Xander listen up. You listening?" asks Keith.

"Yep."

"Tomorrow you will leave the house to pick the rings up that you all had made."

"How did you know about that?"

"Focus, Xander. You will get the rings. While you are there you will be taken."

"To where?"

"We believe Norfolk, VA, but we will be tracking you so don't worry about that."

"What aren't you telling me? And telling me not to worry does the exact opposite by the way."

"Once you are inside the expected location and are

given access to their PC, you will download the feed that we discussed."

"The one that allows you to hear the room?"

"Yes, that one. From there you will do as they ask. Likely they will need some shell corporations created and offshore accounts set up. You will comply."

"I've been researching how to do that because it isn't a part of my typical day to day work life. Oh, and before I forget, when the FBI or some other three letter organization comes after me, I want any and all charges cleared for whatever my involvement is with this whole operation."

"It's already been taken care of, along with your juvenile record that was sealed."

I pause briefly, "How did you know about that if it was sealed?"

"One of the three-letter organizations found out about it when they did a deep dive into your background. We do them on everyone we work with, don't get your panties in a bunch, Xander. I will say you showed a love of technology from a very young age. It's pretty impressive that you were only eleven when you were arrested for accessing government information through the Social Security Offices."

"My grandma wasn't receiving her checks anymore. I was trying to figure out why because nobody at that office would help her."

"If I had your extensive knowledge about stuff like that, I probably would have done the same thing, man. I wasn't giving you shit about it."

"What else do I need to know?"

"Two things. First, we are working on another source within the organization, but can't confirm if they will be an asset yet. Second, a member of the Cartel might make an appearance at the location tomorrow. Play it smart tomorrow, kid. The guy they are sending is a bit of a whack job. He's notorious for blowing shit up and leaving bodies in his wake."

"That is very comforting. Potentially meeting a psychopathic pyro. Day made. Where will you all be because so far everything you have told me makes it so I don't want to do this?"

"We will be listening close by. Do you remember the word if things go sideways?"

"Shove your pineapple, Keith."

"See you tomorrow, kid, and again don't tell anyone."

I hang up my call and wonder for a second what I should tell Ems and her family about why I left the room to take a call during our family meeting. I close my eyes briefly, while gathering my thoughts before I head back into the dining room. Fuck! I hate keeping things from her. If I don't do this she will end up in prison or worse. Finishing that last thought, I walk back into the dining room. Immediately Ems looks up at me.

"Everything okay, Xander?"

I tell her about the rings being ready and that I will grab them on my way to Norfolk.

"Norfolk? Why would you be heading to Norfolk?"

I remember our conversation from the other day about a potential client and decide to go with that.

"The program has to be done tomorrow?"

Of course, Uncle Paul asks about it as well.

"Unfortunately, yes. I know I don't have the family's military background, but I shouldn't be long. I'll have my phone on me the entire time. Would you all feel better if I shared my location?"

A resounding "YES" is heard from the family surrounding the dining room table.

While laughing I tell them, "Okay, I will share it with you all if that will help ease your concern."

Keith is not going to like this, but this family won't let this happen any other way I'm sure of it. He will have to deal with it.

They seem to be accepting of this compromise as Maverick turns the conversation to Mel and Evelyn's plan to evade anyone outside our circle.

We talk about the plan to track and capture Abbott. Maverick and Ems take turns explaining theories and coming to a resolution for the Navy version of capture the flag, only in this scenario, Abbott is the flag.

It's unsettling to know that tomorrow the opposing team will have me as well while this plan is going down. For the remainder of dinner, I pick at my food. I've lost my appetite thinking about tomorrow and the hundreds of ways this can go sideways. I keep stealing glances of Ems. God, she is so smart and has the biggest heart of anyone I know. It hurts my heart to not tell her about this. One day I hope she forgives me.

EMILY

Xander and I start to clean up after dinner after we have said our goodbyes to the family. He closes and locks the door then starts to head upstairs.

"I think that went as well as we could have expected," he states.

"Maybe you could postpone that job tomorrow and wait until this blows over?"

"Ems, I will be fine and only be gone for a few hours. Please don't dwell on this."

I meet him at the top of the stairs and wrap my arms around his waist while placing my head on his chest.

"You are right. I'm being ridiculous. With everything going on, I prefer the thought of you being far away from any potential danger that's all. I'm not sure what this commercial property has to do with anything but tomorrow I hope to get more answers. One way or another, that is. After Mav grabs Abbott, it will finally be time to see what he has been hiding or what he knows."

"Now I'm the one concerned, Ems. You and Mav sure about this plan?"

"As sure as I am that one day soon, I'm going to be your wife, Xander Ellis."

He lifts me up and I wrap my legs around his waist as he walks me back to our bed.

"Say that again."

"One day soon I will be your wife."

Slowly, he lays me down as he places kisses along my neck and down my chest. I arch my back a bit to encourage him to keep going. He grabs my hips and pulls me to him. For a brief moment I think back to the other night when the attacker did a similar motion. I raise myself off the bed and push Xander onto his back. I need to take control to wipe that memory from my mind. As I lean down, I start kissing Xander passionately while I straddle him so I can feel him harden against me. He increases our kissing as he begins to remove my clothes. Leaving kisses where my clothes once were, we stop long enough to remove our pants. Before he can switch positions, I quickly sink down onto him.

"Christ, Ems," he groans as he sits up and squeezes my ass to encourage the movement I've started doing.

My breath catches as I feel us both starting to build up to a release. Wrapping my hands behind his neck, I move my fingers through his dark hair and lightly drag my nails down his back, bringing him even closer to me. He moves to a more seated position as I move my legs around his torso. Placing my hands on the bed behind me, I arch my back enough to take him even deeper. He trails his hands up my back and wraps them into my hair, pulling it slightly causing me to moan with excitement. He speeds up our movement, bringing us to the edge. As our bodies find a rhythm, I kiss him long and slow. I pull away enough to suck his bottom lip, as I feel us both let go.

My body shudders from the intensity of our climax as I

collapse down onto him. He kisses my forehead and whispers, "I love you so much, Emily Fallon, marry me two weeks from today. I don't want to wait. That should give us enough time to get the license and for my parents to get here. I'll call my parents tomorrow. We will get married on the beach or hell the backyard, just say yes, and marry me."

"Xander, I would marry you tonight if all of our loved ones were here. Well, not at this particular moment. Two weeks it is. Call your parents tomorrow." I snuggle up even closer to him to kiss him one more time, before I take those words and his tight embrace and drift off to sleep.

XANDER

My mind won't shut off about the events that are about to occur tomorrow. All of the inner turmoil of not telling Em about Keith's plan or even that I met him continues to build. Looking over at her while she sleeps, a calmness comes over me. I know everything will be okay. It has to be, right? I grab my phone to text my parents.

This deserves much more than a text, but it's late so calling at this hour is out. Ems and I are getting married two weeks from today. We are having a simple ceremony here in the Outer Banks. We would love for you to join us. Feel free to stay at the house in Manteo as I've moved in with Em. Love you both.

I pull her closer to me and mold the front of my body to the back of hers. She stirs a bit but I feel her quickly relax again as she continues to sleep. Holding her this way helps me to finally fall asleep.

* * *

"*Xander*, I can't move."

I wake up to Ems trying to get out of my hold. She tells me my arms kept getting tighter and tighter around her. Almost python like.

"I'm sorry, I guess in my dreams I also don't want to let you go too far from me."

She playfully smacks my arm before she gets up to get ready for her run. Looking over at the clock, I see that I managed a whole two hours of sleep. With that, I let out a groan. It's going to be a long day.

We go for our run and complete it in record time. Once we are home, she heads off to shower and prepare for her workday/kidnapping of Abbott while I make us some breakfast.

"I'll take one of those," she says as she snatches a piece of bacon from the plate and hops onto the counter to keep me company for the last few minutes while I finish making our food.

"I was thinking about our song. What do you think it should be? I have one song in my mind, but it isn't really a typical wedding song."

"We could pick something from our playlist that we've made through the years."

"Oh, the one I have in mind is on there," she laughs.

"Now I want to know what you have in mind."

She begins laughing and hits play on her phone. Hootie and the Blowfish "Only Wanna Be with You" starts playing throughout the kitchen.

"Well, we did love this song when we were younger."

"I think it's perfect for us and it isn't a traditional wedding song which makes me love it even more."

"I think it's a great choice, babe."

* * *

After I assemble our plates and set them on the breakfast bar, I maneuver myself between her legs to block her from jumping down from the counter.

"Ready for another go at it, babe?"

"Ems, I'm always ready to go again."

"It's going to have to wait until tonight, I'm afraid. We both have a busy day and Maverick will be waiting for me at the station."

I slide my hands under her bottom and pull her to me then carry her to her seat at the breakfast bar so she can eat before she has to leave. I kiss her temple before I completely let go of her and she turns her head up with the sweetest smile that melts my heart.

Fuck you Keith for not letting me tell her, I think to myself.

We make small talk and plans for dinner tonight to hopefully celebrate a victory of getting information from Abbott. She finishes her food and grabs some coffee for her drive.

"Ems?"

"What's up, Xander?"

"Nothing, I wanted to tell you that I love you, you are incredible, and I will see you later tonight."

"Maybe we should order food in so clothes can be optional?"

"God woman, you have to stop saying stuff like that or we will never leave this house."

She laughs, winks at me then turns toward the garage door to leave. Before walking through it, she blows me a kiss.

After cleaning up from breakfast, I grab my backpack and place my laptop inside. The note that was left at our door falls to the floor. Quickly, I grab it and throw it in the bag. What do you bring with you when you know you are about to be kidnapped? I head over to the pantry to grab some snacks. Once I feel content, I quickly shower so I can head to Kill Devil Hills to pick up the rings and prepare to be taken.

I park my car toward the end of the lot near the back. *This looks like a good spot to be kidnapped from* I think to myself. My reflexes tell me to lock the door but a little voice tells me to leave them alone. With that, I head inside to pick up the rings.

* * *

"Good morning, Sir. How may I help you today?" the jeweler inquires.

It's the same man that helped us the other day.

"I'm here to pick up the two rings that were said to be ready."

"What name would they be under?"

"Emily Fallon, my fiancée."

"Oh, I remember this order now. She didn't want you to see yours with the engraving right?"

"That's right, but I promise I won't look."

The clerk laughs and hands me one box that holds Emily's wedding band and another box that's wrapped with paper.

"This one that is wrapped is yours."

"Clever, but what's keeping me from just taking the paper off?"

"I met your fiancée; she seems like a pistol. Personally, I wouldn't want to anger her."

Laughing at his very solid point, I respond with, "You are not wrong." I gather both boxes and thank him for his time.

As I walk back to my car I try not to look around. It's quite difficult knowing you will be eventually taken but not knowing when is awful. Ignoring the jeweler's comments, I rip the paper off the box that holds my ring. I still haven't looked at the engraving; instead, I place our rings in my pocket and climb into my car.

"Place your hands on the wheel and listen very closely," a voice from the backseat tells me, as he holds cold metal against the side of my neck. I assume it's a gun, so I do as I'm told.

"You will drive until I tell you to stop. If you do as you are told, everything will be fine."

I nod my head to reflect my understanding.

"Head to Norfolk."

My passenger doesn't talk almost the entire trip. I try to steal glances in the rearview mirror. His dark buzz cut hairstyle and his athletic build tells me he's definitely in the Navy. Just making sure I didn't get taken by the wrong bad guy.

"Go past the station entrances. A few blocks down there will be a restaurant up on your left that sits in a lot by itself. Across the street on the right is another vacant building. Pull into the lot on the right."

"Got it," I reply and do as directed.

Once we get to the lot, my passenger exits the vehicle first but quickly opens my door.

"Undo your seatbelt and get out of the car. If you try to run, I will shoot you right here."

While I don't think he will, I'm not about to play a game with him to find out. Once I'm out of the car we move around the building and start to head across the street. The passenger said it was a restaurant. Maverick and Emily mentioned something about Abbott purchasing a restaurant. They are planning to grab Abbott today and likely from this restaurant. How am I going to explain this? Assuming I get out of this, I'll make Keith explain it to her. That way she can take it out on him.

We head into the front door of the old restaurant. It appears to be abandoned standing alone away from other buildings on the block. From the outside, it looks much bigger. Inside it's basically two rooms. The main dining area and the kitchen. I probably shouldn't be too surprised that it looks almost identical to the one I met Keith at the other day. I'm sure back in the day this restaurant would draw in locals and tourists alike. You can almost picture the patrons off to the left side of the main room clinking glasses, drinking cocktails, and laughing while they wait for their food. Unbeknownst to them, one day this place would be vacant. Now it belongs to Abbott and his creepy men.

My captor walks me to the connected room and in where appliances once were is a metal table and two chairs. On the table is a computer.

"Have a seat," he says, as he points to the chair.

Once seated, he slides me a piece of paper that has a login and password on it along with directions.

Xander, comply with our requests and you will be set free in a few hours with the understanding that you will not talk to anyone about what you are about to do. Remember we are always watching. If you tell anyone or try to alert anyone, you will be shot by my friend who brought you here.

Your objective is to create two shell companies. From there you will also create four offshore accounts. The computer provided has already been set up for you. You will need to shield your location as you work. I'm sure someone with your experience won't have a problem with this.

The instructions end there. I look at my captor for any further directions.

"Get started," he orders.

Once I log in, I set the program to allow the room to be heard first. Then I provide a way to bounce my location all over the world to avoid being tracked. From there, I begin the setup of the shell companies and offshore accounts. My hand gravitates to my pocket to feel the two rings reminding me why I agreed to do this.

My captor seems oblivious to anything I'm doing when I ask him for a pen and paper.

"I need it to write down the account and routing numbers."

He grunts and leaves the room briefly. He walks back in a few moments later with a pen and a couple of sticky notes and tells me, "Write small, this is all I could find."

I begin to write down the shell company info and the first few account and routing numbers for the offshore accounts.

"Someone will need to make a deposit into each of these. It doesn't have to be huge, but I need to make sure they are receiving wires correctly."

He reaches for his phone to make a call then leaves the room again.

He reappears after a few minutes to tell me that someone will be here soon to help with that.

So, we wait.

ABBOTT

*A*fter dropping off a package for my family at the Post Office, my phone ringing brings me back to reality. For a moment I pictured my life with Maria and Miggy far from here. Somewhere nobody would find us. Somewhere safe.

"Make it quick," I command.

"The guy says he needs someone to make a deposit into the accounts. Nothing big but he needs to make sure they are working correctly."

"Is he done yet?"

"Almost."

"I'll head that way."

I make another quick call.

"Abbott, what do you have for me?"

"It's starting. The kid is at the restaurant."

"Heard that. Remember what we discussed. You are up."

"I know. I want this over. Whatever it takes."

"That's the plan. I'll check back in a bit."

Ending the call, I grab my keys, head out of the station to my car, and off to the restaurant.

EMILY

*A*fter I park in my usual spot, I head inside to my office where I'm greeted by Maverick.

"Well, hello, brother."

He shuts the door behind me.

"You ready for today, Emme?"

"I am. With our plan, I feel like it's going to be a good day. Oh, block your calendar for two weeks from yesterday. Xander and I picked a date for the wedding."

"Remind me when this is over because you know Mel is the one to keep track of all of this."

"I will remind you, don't worry. Did Mel and Evelyn begin their journey yet?

"Yes, this morning. The sooner we wrap this up the better. Let's go over it one more time. If Abbott leaves the station today, I will follow him, grab him, and take him to the agreed upon location for questioning using whatever tactics are needed to get the info."

"Did you check his location today?"

"I did and he beat me to work today. He's been here

since early this morning. The app will alert us if he leaves this spot."

Almost as if it heard us talking about it, we receive a text from the app notifying us that he is on the move.

"He's leaving. Stay here and I will message after I have him."

"Mav, watch your back and stay safe."

"Emme, this is what I do, but I love that you worry about me still."

He walks out of my office and that's when my nerves begin. *I almost lost him last year. Maybe I should go as his backup. No, he's right, he does this for a living. He will be fine.* I think to myself.

Trying to keep myself busy, I review more service reports for the ships in port. My mind is not focused on work right now.

My phone alerts me to an incoming text after ten minutes have passed. "Good God that was quick," I tell myself as I reach for my phone.

It's from Mav.

Emme, we have a problem.

My stomach sinks after reading those words. I respond back with a question mark.

Mav: Xander's car is here across from the place I followed Abbott to. Check his location. I'm dropping my pin so you can compare.

I open my messages from Xander and select his contact info to track his location. Fighting the urge to vomit, I text Maverick back.

Me: It's him.

Mav: Plans changed. Get here now. I'm about a half mile from the restaurant. It's a quick jog over but this location has a great area to hide our vehicles. I sent you my pin.

I fly out of my office and sprint to Katniss. Panic ensues as my mind races. What is he doing there? Is this a joke? Did Abbott set him up? He must have, right? Xander wouldn't have met him willingly without telling any of us. I run red lights trying to get to the pinned location as quickly as I can. Please don't let someone try and pull me over. Today is not the day to mess with me.

I'm parking next to Maverick's car within minutes calling him as I exit the vehicle.

"Where are you? I'm with your car."

"I'm at the restaurant trying to get an idea of what's going on."

"On my way." Quickly, I end the call and run toward the restaurant, keeping my head on a swivel to make sure I'm not being followed. I can see Mav ahead; he's leaning against one of the exterior walls on the backside of the restaurant.

Once I catch up with him, he asks me, "What's the new plan, Emme?"

"We call this thing off with Abbott for now and grab my fiancé."

"I like the new plan. Let's go."

We quickly talk about access points into the building and decide to divide and conquer. Maverick starts to hand me his gun from his ankle, but I stop him because I have mine from my nightstand. As we get closer to the building, we hear a car approach the back side of the old restaurant. We can hear four car doors close right around the corner from where we are standing. Maverick signals for me to stay put and listen. A voice with a thick accent starts to speak, "Take that, get out of sight, and wait for my order."

We both shrug our shoulders at each other because we don't recognize the voice. We decide to sit tight hoping to not be seen.

ABBOTT

"Where is he?"

"In the back, Sir, finishing up the accounts."

I walk into the connected back room and see Xander working away on the computer.

"You ready to test the accounts?"

The kid looks at me over the computer.

"Abbott, I should have known you were behind all of this."

"Look, kid, this isn't personal. You have a unique skill set and honestly, I'm surprised you haven't been taken before now."

"Well, that's comforting."

"What do you need from me to move this forward?"

He slides the four account numbers and routing numbers to the other side of the table for me to review.

"You need to make a deposit, any amount is fine, but I need to check the accounts to make sure they are transmitting and receiving properly."

I set up a wire transfer to the first account and hit send.

"$100k. I'm glad to see you chose a small amount like I suggested," he replies.

"Safe to assume the other three are fine now?"

"Sure. Am I free to go now?"

"Not yet. You've proven to be useful. I think I will keep you until our out-of-town friend arrives. He's on his way now."

I hear the door behind me open and an older gentleman wearing an expensive suit walks in. That must be Gabriel who is flanked by two very large men who are also in nice suits. I've been told by Stanley that Gabriel is a psychopath. If he doesn't like something he literally will pulverize it and move on. Let's hope this is a quick visit and up to his standards or we all might not leave this room.

"Who is this?" asks the older gentleman.

"This is our computer specialist. Don't worry about him."

"So, he is expendable, no?"

"No, he isn't. We need him, for now."

I look over at the kid and I see his chest relax like he had been holding his breath.

"Where are we with my new American business venture, Abbott?"

"He is finishing up the accounts now. I've sent a deposit to check the workability. All is good, we are on track."

"And this is the business you are using to clean my money? Looks a bit run down."

"We will have it up and running quickly, Gabriel."

"This won't do. I needed this up and running a week ago. You failed me, Abbott." He turns to his men and says, "Once this guy is done, kill him and these two then have Marco blow the building."

"That's not necessary. We can use this for storage for

now while we look into other business opportunities. There are businesses for sale all over the place."

"You had all sorts of time, Abbott, to make this work. What would you do in my position?"

I look around the room trying to buy some time before answering, "I would make this work. It has potential. Your operation is going to expand quickly here. We will need this location. I'm sure of it. Let's start with this location and in a month, when you have doubled your profits, we will expand to another location. Give me two weeks."

The look on Gabriel's face as he looks around looks less than convinced, has me worried.

"Something feels off. Are you trying to set me up, Abbott? Do I look like a fool to you?"

"Gabriel, I wouldn't do that. We have had a long-standing relationship with the Cartel. For years we have helped you evade getting caught. Why would that change now? We are all excited about you expanding to the US."

"I don't trust you. Never have. Why did Stanley stop meeting with us?"

"He was promoted. That made it difficult for him to get away to meet you. He trusted me with that duty and I have been faithful to you and the Cartel for years. Nobody is trying to set you up."

"I don't buy your act, Abbott."

He looks at his men and says, "Do as I say and kill Abbott first, then his guard, then the computer guy."

From behind me, I hear the chair scoot out quickly and the kid starts to yell.

"Hey, excuse me, Mr. Drug Lord, look I've done what you've asked and I can help you move your money, but I can't do that if I'm dead. I'll be a worthless pineapple."

Did he say pineapple? Oh, fuck is that some sort of safe word? Dammit, here we go. I think to myself.

Within seconds the room fills with smoke from someone throwing in smoke grenades for a distraction. I move quickly toward the kid because he's a loose end. Gunfire starts to ring out through the small area. I pull my weapon and continue moving towards the table. The smoke hasn't started to dissipate yet, but as I reach and feel for the table, I can tell that Xander is no longer sitting at it.

I hear Gabriel yell something but I can't quite make it out. The last thing I hear him say is "Marco, blow the building now."

The door behind me locks as I continue to sweep the room trying to find the kid. It's impossible to see through this dense smoke.

"Xander!" I yell but I get no response from him. Fuck. "Kid, are you in here? I'm trying to help you here. You are better off with me if you are trying to pick a side." No response. I've swept the room as much as I could under the circumstances, and I clearly heard Gabriel give the order to blow the building. I tried to save him but I'm not going out like this. I head to the front of the restaurant and trip over something. Bending down to see what I tripped on, I feel an arm. The smoke is so thick I can't see anything even right in front of me. I follow the arm with my fingers until I feel the wrist joint. I check for a pulse; there isn't one. Fuck, they already took him out. Feeling around on the floor near the arm, I try to look for the pieces of paper he was writing on but my fingers hit something small. Running my hands over the ground carefully I feel two small circular metal items. They aren't what I'm looking for so I leave them.

Time to get out of here, there's nothing else I can do. Feeling for the front door, I break through it and start running toward my car when I'm tackled from behind.

"Stay the fuck down," a voice yells at me as a gun is shoved onto the back of my head.

"Okay, Okay."

My arms are pulled behind my back and my wrists are zip-tied. I'm abruptly brought to my feet and confronted by my opponent.

"Maverick?"

"Shut up and get in the fucking car."

He opens the back door of my car and shoves me in. He must have grabbed my keys when he tackled me because he slams the door and starts the car up. In the passenger seat is Emily Fallon.

"Where is, Xander, you piece of shit?"

"He is in the building still. I tried to find him but I think the Cartel took him out. I tripped over a body on my way out while I was looking for him. I checked for a pulse but there wasn't one." As I finish that comment a loud explosion happens behind us. I turn in my seat to see what's left of the building that's now engulfed in flames. Something struck the restaurant's aging structure, embedding itself within its walls.

"Maverick, stop the fucking car!" Emily screams.

"Looks like they cleaned up their mess."

"I will shoot you where you sit if you don't shut the fuck up."

Maverick stops the car, opens my door, grabs my shirt, and pulls me to him. That's all I remember.

EMILY

*T*wenty minutes earlier.

*A*fter the three voices enter the building. Maverick and I think of a contingency plan. Now there are at least four people inside not including Xander. We have no idea how many others might be in there. Four would be easy to take out but not knowing about others makes us take a step back.

"We should breach from the front of the building, Emme. Go in together and sweep through the building clearing rooms as we go."

"I like the new plan."

As we move our way to the front end of the building, we hear another car pull up. We both flatten ourselves against the wall. We hear multiple car doors again. This time there isn't any talking.

I whisper to Maverick, "What is going on here?"

He shrugs because neither of us has any idea about who's in this building now.

"New plan, we wait for Abbott to come out. We grab him and then get Xander after that. He's smart, he will figure out how to get out if the opportunity presents itself."

I don't like this plan but we have no clue what we are up against now. I begrudgingly agree. We head toward Abbott's car. Maverick stops halfway and tells me to head to his car and he's going to wait near one of the other vehicles. That way if he comes out, he can tackle him and restrain him as originally planned. We don't have many options now, so I continue to the vehicle and Mav waits crouched down near a black SUV.

Once I'm in the car, I look back to the building at the same time Abbott takes off running from the front door. I see Mav spot him and tackle him like a damn linebacker. He gets him to his feet and into the back of the car.

"Where is Xander, asshole?"

"He is in the building still. I tried to find him but I think the Cartel took him out. I tripped over a body on my way out while I was looking for him. I checked for a pulse but there wasn't one."

There's a deafening explosion so powerful that it rattles the windows and the entirety of the car. My ears are ringing. I see the building behind us now engulfed in flames with a large opening where a wall once was.

"Maverick, stop the fucking car!"

"Looks like they cleaned up their mess," states Abbott.

"I will shoot you where you sit if you don't shut the fuck up."

Now the building Xander is in is consumed by fire. Maverick pulls the car over, gets out, and pistol whips Abbott with his gun knocking him out.

I take off in a sprint to the building. When I reach what's left, I try to get close enough to go in.

"Emily. What are you doing? You can't go in there."

"Maverick, you heard him. Xander is in there."

"I know but if you go in there you will die."

"I have to get to him, Maverick."

"Do you hear that? The sirens? We have to go right now, Emme!"

The fiery inferno increases like an insatiable hunger as it consumes the building. The heat coming off it is painful as close as we are standing to it. The pungent smell of the smoke fills the air leaving a bitter taste in my mouth.

Maverick yelling at me brings me back to reality, "We need to leave right now or we won't be able to end this. We have Abbott, we need to go."

I know what he's saying makes sense, but I don't care. I continue to try to find a way in as I begin to yell for him. "Xander!"

No response

"Xander!"

No response.

The sirens are getting closer. The roaring from the blaze continues.

"Dammit, Emily, we have to go right now! Don't make me subdue you to get you in the damn car."

"FUCK! Maverick, I will never forgive you for making me leave him here."

"Emme, you are making me choose between ending this once and for all, my family, or finding out what we already know. Now get in the damn car."

I hear what he's saying but I won't leave him here. I take off toward the building again at the same time another explosion rocks the building, shaking it to its foundation. The front doorway is obliterated, flames are now pouring out where a door once was. The blast forced us back several feet and knocks us to the ground. My ears are ringing, my head is pounding, tears are streaming down my face. There's this horrible blood-curdling scream that I hear in the distance. Someone picks me up off the ground and I realize we are running now.

The building's façade starts to crumble, revealing the skeletal remains of what once was. The bricks that were sturdy and steadfast, now lay scattered like fallen soldiers. Their surfaces are charred from the destructive power of the explosion. The screaming is getting louder.

Maverick tosses me into the front seat. When I start to comprehend what's happening. I realize the blood curdling scream is coming from me.

I'm screaming because Xander was in the building that is now a pile of rubble. My body starts to convulse from the emotions flowing through me. I'm shaking uncontrollably. I look around the car trying to focus on something familiar, noticing that Abbott is still knocked out in the backseat. Maverick floors the gas and we race away from the restaurant. Maverick tells me that he saw a glimpse of the fire truck and a police car in the rearview mirror as he turned the corner.

Looking behind us as we speed away, the glow of the fire can be seen for blocks. The embers dance through the air. The old restaurant or what's left of it now stands as a tragic symbol of destruction and loss. My loss.

I stare blankly out of my window as we head to a warehouse that Uncle Paul owns. Maverick is talking to me but I'm not hearing anything he's saying. My mind keeps seeing the building going up in flames. The hole in the side of it looked like something out of an old war movie. What caused that damage? Where did it come from? Who else was in that building when it went up? Why was there a second explosion?

I'm not sure how much time has passed or how long we've been driving.

We pull up to the warehouse, but I stay in the car for a bit. Abbott is starting to come too. Maverick pulls him from the vehicle and walks him inside. Uncle Paul comes to my side of the car and opens my door. "Emily, you need to come inside. It isn't safe for you out here right now."

My head shakes from side to side but my body follows my uncle's request and exits the car.

Once inside the building, I begin to pace back and forth. This can't be happening; he has to be alright. Maybe he was somewhere in the building that was a pocket or safe room when the explosions happened. Uncle Paul stops in front of me to end my pacing, pulls me to him to hug me and tells me to take deep breaths.

"Can you tell me what happened, Emily?"

"We heard people go in, but we are unsure about the number. There were five people for sure, maybe more," I ramble on to him.

"Did you all see anyone leave the building?"

I'm not sure I answer him. My mind keeps replaying the explosion over and over again like some fucked up loop. I can't unsee it. It's being etched into my mind. This day I will never forget. Add this to the list of memories I wish I could stop seeing. The day my dad left for his last deployment. David left to go hiking without me because I messed up my ankle and he was murdered by Asher. My mom dying of a broken heart not too long after that while I was deployed. Now Xander, taken before I had the chance to save him. Could I have saved all of them? Is this my fault? Are all of their deaths on my hands?

"Emily? Can you hear me?"

My mind is numb along with my whole body.

"Emily, have a seat. I'm going to try and get an update."

I hear him leave the room. I'm not sure how long he is gone before he returns. There is no way I can sit right now. I'm frozen in this one spot in this one room.

My uncle's face is tense. His eyebrows are furrowed. His eyes look heavy and sad. As he begins to speak, his voice quivers a bit, "Emily, they found one person, deceased. They can't tell anything about the person due to the extreme heat of the fire. Someone must have used a missile or something similar to cause that amount of damage that quickly."

I hear words being delivered deliberately and slowly. The air in this space begins to feel somber. There's a palpable tension that hangs in the room as he continues to talk to me but the only word I heard was deceased.

"No. No. No. No. No." I collapse to the ground.

"Emily, we don't know it's him. Stay with me."

Uncle Paul pulls me into a connected room with a couch and some chairs. He directs me to one of the chairs to have a seat.

"I'm going to get you some water and see if I can find out some more information. I'll be right back."

He leaves the room and all I can do is think about me leaving Xander in that building. Maverick could have left with Abbott and left me there. Maybe I should go back. Answer any questions that the authorities might have about the building or who might be inside. I get up to start to leave when Uncle Paul comes back into the room with a bottle of water.

"It isn't much, but I have some news. They have labeled it a criminal bombing from the preliminary evaluation of the scene. The bomb squad, ATF, and the local first responders are there securing the scene while looking for other potential threats. There were two explosions. They added a statement that no survivors were discovered at the scene. One body was recovered along with some items that are being logged for evidence. I will keep you updated as much as possible, Emily."

My entire body feels nothing. My thoughts are racing. Time feels like it has completely stopped. I think I nodded with understanding, but I don't know. My movements don't feel like my own anymore.

Uncle Paul pulls me up into the tightest hug he has ever given me. It was then that I knew what he already knew. The body mentioned earlier. Body means someone who is no longer living. The body is Xander. I quickly push away from him and start to vomit. The breakfast he made us this morning now sits on the floor at my feet.

At first, disbelief is what I feel. It feels like time is paused trapping me in this moment of agony. The weight of the news crushes me, making it hard to breathe. The love of my life, best friend, my person, my fiancé is gone. The pounding in my head won't stop. I feel lightheaded, my legs give out and then everything goes black.

EMILY

I feel someone nudging me.

"Emily, I need you to wake up and drink some water."

In the aftermath of the news I was given, a profound sense of emptiness surrounds me.

My eyes flutter open. I look around the room I'm in to see that it's a room I barely recognize. There's the couch I'm lying on, a desk, and a few chairs. It's the room from earlier.

"I need you to drink this please."

He hands me a large glass of ice water that I take and empty its contents to comfort the dryness of my throat. It's so dry like I haven't drank water in days. I remember why my throat is dry. From my screaming. And I was screaming because Xander is gone. The events from earlier come crashing back. It had to be a dream but it's a nightmare. My nightmare that Xander is really gone.

Throwing off the small blanket someone put over me, I jump from the bed and push past Uncle Paul to leave the room.

"Emily, where are you going? You need to lie down; you might have a concussion from the blast."

"I'm fine. Where is he? Where's Abbott?"

"Maverick has him in another room and has been questioning him for the past several hours. I text Maverick to let him know you are awake now."

"I need to see Abbott. Now."

"Maverick is handling it, Emily. You need to rest. You are in shock and need to take some time."

"No, I've moved passed that to pissed the fuck off. I need to find out who killed Xander and that starts with talking to Abbott."

He grabs my arms to hold me in place as I begin to fight against his grip. But he pulls me into an almost crushing bear hug.

"Emily, please stop fighting; I need you to hear me. Maverick is questioning him and you need to take a beat here."

The weight of my body becomes too much as my legs start to give out. I think back to Xander. His smile, those dimples, his arms holding me. None of it will ever happen again. I will never see him again. My uncle helps me to the couch. This immense anger is building inside. I need to get out of here, I feel like I can't breathe. It's like I'm suffocating. Pulling together my remaining energy, I bolt towards the door of the room I'm in. It opens up to a larger empty room. Across the way is another door. I take off toward it.

Once outside, I stop. Looking around, I realize I'm not sure where we are. I can hear the water but can't see it. There are smaller buildings next to the one we are in. Nothing looks familiar at all. Uncle Paul follows me through the door.

"Emily, come back inside. We are going to be here for a bit."

"Where are we?"

"In a warehouse that a friend of mine owns near the station."

"I need to go back to the house. There are things there I need to grab."

"We won't be going back to the houses. People have been there looking for us. They've been completely tossed. For now, we are safer here."

Thinking about the fact that I won't be able to go back to the last place I saw Xander alive hits me. The crying begins and the sobbing racks my body. The questions start to go through my mind again. *Why was he in Norfolk? Who was this new job with? Did Abbott set him up? Why Xander? Why didn't they come after Maverick, Uncle Paul, or myself?* These are the questions that only Abbott can answer.

"I had someone go to your house to grab a few things for you. I also asked them to grab Xander's PC, but it wasn't there. The entire house was turned upside down. Somebody is looking for something."

"Where are our vehicles?"

"Still at the place you and Mav met at earlier. Emily, I know you need answers. We all do. But I need you to trust me that my people are looking into this from many angles and Maverick is doing everything he can to get answers from Abbott. You need your rest. Please know we are doing everything we can to get answers."

"Your everything isn't good enough." I push past him and try to take his keys in the process. He quickly turns to grab my arm applying slight pressure. I start to hit him in the chest. I know the blows aren't hurting him because he's one of the toughest men I know. He grabs my other arm and tries to restrain me a bit. Continuing to fight against him, my energy feels depleted being held in place. I fall into him and start to cry again.

"Emily, you want answers. We all do. We will get them but you need to take a moment to rest please."

"I will rest when I'm dead. Like Xander is. Right now, I want to see Abbott. You need to let me see him. That isn't a question that is my demand, Uncle."

"You have your mother's fight in you, my dear, and your father's persistence. A true Fallon if I ever saw one. I will take you to see him."

"That's what I need right now. Thank you."

"You know, Emily, your burning rage might be what's needed to get some answers. Abbott has had this coming to him for years. I'm not going to fight you on this."

He extends his arm toward the door and encourages me to walk back into the building. Once inside, I follow him through the empty room and into another one.

The rage inside me builds. I hear statements being made trying to get my mind to focus on something else but I ignore them. He sounds like the character from Charlie Brown that doesn't make any sense just sounds. There is only one thing on my mind right now. Eye for eye. Abbott woke a beast inside me when he took my person from me. Now he will have to pay.

ABBOTT

I know how this will end. Now that the tables have turned, they won't stop until they have all the answers they have been searching for. The room I'm in is dimly lit. The air is heavy. Maverick's gaze is piercing, and his expression reflects his determination to get answers.

Maverick hits me again. He's been at this for over an hour and yet he doesn't seem to tire from the physical exertion. Unlike my face that feels every last punch.

"I didn't want to turn into the monster that I was in that room with last year. We called him the muscle, not sure what his name actually was nor do I care. Do you know who I'm referring to? The one that murdered O'Shea. But you aren't leaving me much of a choice here, Abbott. Being in that room last year taught me a few lessons on persuasion that the Navy doesn't teach you. Before we resort to those, though, I have a few ideas of my own."

He walks to the opposite side of the room where a table sits. On the table are tools, a car battery device used to shock people, jumper cables, and some additional items that I can't quite make out. He brings the battery and cables over and sets them near me.

"Whatever I do to you now, will be much nicer compared to what my sister will do if she finds you in here."

I know all he wants is the truth about what happened with the Xander kid but I can only tell him what I know.

"I've told you what happened while I was in the old restaurant. He was there at the table and then he wasn't. I came across a body on my way out. I checked for a pulse and he was gone."

He attaches the cable to the battery device that looks like it's connected to something else to give it even more voltage and then to me. His words have been carefully chosen, designed to lure me into a trap. He's hoping to expose the truth hidden behind years of deceit.

"Who did this?"

He turns on the device to send me a significant jolt. My teeth instantly clench, my muscles contract and spasm. He turns it off.

"The Cartel from Ecuador. The individual that made an appearance, his name is Gabriel. He is in charge of all the drug runs that we help them with. He didn't like the way the operation was going up to this point. He's a bit of a control freak and pulls the trigger, for lack of a better term, rather quickly in most cases. In this case, he wanted all of us dead and the building to be blown. He thought I was setting him up and wouldn't listen to reason."

He sends another voltage through the device. This one was a bit stronger.

I start to convulse a bit and feel my hands flex causing them to pull on the restraints holding me in place. He turns it off when he's satisfied.

"Where was Xander during this?"

"He was at a table setting up offshore accounts for the Cartel."

Another surge is sent through. Now I'm getting pissed off. "Fucking stop, I'm telling you the truth, Maverick."

He ends the voltage.

"Who hired him?"

"I had him kidnapped by my lacky, Pierce. Who must have escaped or was taken."

"So, Xander didn't know about any of this?"

He doesn't send a surge this time. Maybe he's realizing my answers haven't changed from the first three times he asked me the same questions.

"I didn't say that. He made a comment right before everything went south. One that made me think he was using a safe word as if he was working for someone."

"Who the hell would he be working with, Abbott?"

He sends another surge. So much for thinking that was done. He still doesn't believe my answers. Can't say that I blame him, he has zero reason to trust me. He ends the surge. My body is physically exhausted from the beating and now the shocks from the battery device.

The door to the warehouse opens and a very pissed-off Fallon walks in. Maverick tries to block her path.

"Emme, I'm handling it."

"Maverick, move out of my way before I hurt you."

"Emme, he's talking. Let me finish this."

"He's lying, Maverick, he won't give you any information. Not without an ulterior motive."

"You are in shock. You can't be trusted with him right now."

"He murdered our family and Xander. He doesn't deserve to be shown any mercy."

"I'm shocking him with battery cables, Emme, I'm not

showing him mercy. Let me finish this and we can talk."

She manages to get past Maverick. She is a sly one. She sends a quick round kick to my face followed by a quick move to the neck knocking the wind out of me. I guess I had that coming for kidnapping her man.

"Emme! You have to let me do this for you. This isn't you and I don't want you to live with the choices you want to make in the state you are in. This is my job. My moral compass left years ago. I will make him pay. Please trust me."

Paul walks in shortly as Maverick's comment begins to resonate with Fallon. It's his turn to question me it would appear.

"Ted Abbott. Quite the predicament we have here. In all the years I've known you, I never thought you would sell your soul to make a quick buck."

"Old friend it's interesting to discover the lengths you will go to when a proper paycheck is dangled in front of you. The only reason why you are still alive is that you were the small fish in the grand scheme of things. Mike was the problem and was taken care of."

With that comment, Emily sends another kick to my face and pushes the button on the battery device to send another jolt. The electricity rips through my body. She doesn't turn it off like Maverick did before. I'm uncontrollably shaking, my muscles tensing up, my heart is racing and pounding in my chest. The world around me starts to blur as I feel like my bladder is going to fail on me soon if the connection isn't stopped. Maverick quickly ends the connection and tells her again to let him finish this.

The blind rage in her eyes is honorable and if I weren't her target, I would be impressed. Paul steps between Emily and I to provide a barrier.

"In the office now, please," Maverick tells them.

EMILY

The burning fire that is tearing through my body creates a rage that is unfamiliar to me the moment I see Abbott sitting chained to that chair. The round kick I got in was a cheap shot but for a moment I felt something. The feeling was fleeting. I start to wonder if I will ever feel it again. Right now, I'm trying to shut my emotions off because I can't feel the pain of losing Xander. There will be time for that when this is all over. Now is the time to get the answers we have been looking for. Now is the time to make Abbott pay for the hurt and pain he's caused through the years and for the people he's taken from our lives. The rage builds to an almost blinding effect. I reach for the battery device and crank the knob to send a power surge through him. It takes a minute for Maverick to realize what I've done. Once he does, he begins to lecture me.

Uncle Paul and Maverick guide me to a small office near the main portion of the warehouse. Once inside, Maverick tells us what he's found out up to this point.

"Abbott says he had Xander taken by one of his cronies. A guy named Pierce. He mentioned he isn't sure what happened to Pierce. Either he fled or was taken by the Cartel. They were responsible for the building explosion and he thinks they shot Xander before it blew. He's been pretty forthcoming after a few rounds of punches. When I hooked him to the battery his story didn't change."

"Why is he being so forthcoming, Maverick? He was a trained assassin essentially for the SWCC. After his first wife died, so did the best parts of him. He hasn't had to live by any code other than his own in years. Why start now?" replies Uncle Paul.

"Let me question him, Mav, I need to do this."

"Emily, the look in your eyes right now is not you. You are blinded by rage. You will kill him, and you won't recover from that. You weren't built to take someone's life like this. Doing it for your country or for self-defense because you have to is one thing. Like this is something much darker," explains Maverick.

"Did he say anything else?" asks Uncle Paul.

"He mentioned that he thinks Xander was working for someone. That he possibly mentioned a safe word. Do you know anything about that, Emme?"

"You all heard what he told me."

I have to take a minute to gather my thoughts because my emotions are all over the place right now.

"Xander said he had a new client. That he had to be in Norfolk today to install a program. So, either he knew the client was Abbott or Abbott set him up with the client story and then grabbed him."

"Have you noticed him being off at all lately. Maybe not as outspoken with information or like he had something on his mind?"

"No, we tell each other everything."

"Everything, Emme, you sure about that? Because I know you have withheld items from him in the past."

"For his safety, Maverick, and look where that got us!"

"Emme, that's my point. What if he knew something or was working with someone? Maybe someone threatened you and he did all this to protect you?"

"He would have come to me. I know it." I take a few minutes for myself to think about the last few days with Xander. Last night before everyone came over for dinner, I remember he was spacing off. "There might have been something going on with him yesterday. I was trying to ask him a question and he was completely zoned out. That's not something he does. I should have pushed him for information. Maybe we wouldn't be having this discussion right now."

"Emme, don't do that. This isn't your fault. You can't blame yourself for any of this."

Uncle Paul clears his throat to get our attention.

"Emily, I'm going to go out there and talk to Ted. Him and I go back a long time. Maybe I can play on that and get information from him. My hopes are not high. Like I said, he was a trained assassin, essentially. He turned most of his emotions off years ago."

I nod to him and stay in the office for now. Maverick pulls me into a hug but I don't want to get upset again so I push him away.

"I can't do this right now, Mav. I can't let my emotions take over. I need to block them out until I see this through."

"It's okay to grieve, Emme, you need to."

"Not until this is finished. I will take time after we get what we need."

Maverick and I stay in the office with a deafening silence between us, while our uncle questions Abbott. The clock on the wall reflects that almost forty-five minutes have passed since he went into the warehouse. When Uncle Paul walks back into the office, he has a smirk on his face.

ABBOTT

*P*aul comes out of the office first.

"Ted, what is going on?"

"I told Maverick everything that happened."

"How about you tell me now."

"Fine, I'll back up a few days. You had one of my guys that strayed a bit. His name was Spencer. The one who attacked Fallon. For the record, not that it matters, nobody gave him the order to attack her. My other guy, Pierce, had an item of Spencer's bugged to keep tabs on him because Pierce had a feeling that he would do something stupid. He was right."

"We found the bug."

"Right, but before you destroyed it, we heard him give our names. He was chatting like a damn doll with one of those cords. You know you ask it a question and pull the cord. Anyways, I gave Pierce the order to kill him."

"I know all of this, Ted. Stop wasting my time."

"When things went off the rails, I had to call Robert Stanley and tell him what happened. He told me to make a choice. My options were not ideal but the main one was to speed up the timeline, grab the Xander kid then kill the remaining Fallons. That includes you."

"So, you got the kid and now what, you are planning to kill us?"

"No, that's when I called an audible."

"What does that even mean? Stop talking in riddles and get to the damn point."

"Fine. You knew about the drug runs we've been doing for years. Well, the Cartel wanted to expand their business to the United States. I was tasked with finding a location to clean their money and store their drugs. I needed someone with Xander's understanding of computers to set up some offshore accounts and shell corporations. That's it. Next thing Gabriel, the Cartel contact, is getting a hairy trigger finger and wants us all killed. He thinks it was some sort of elaborate setup for him. He orders his people to kill us and blow the building. The Xander kid makes a plea for his life using this crazy phrase that I can only assume was a safe word provided by the DEA. You know how they are with those things, Paul."

He nods and I continue, "The room filled with smoke and gunfire ensues. I'm trying to find the kid to get him out but he's nowhere to be found."

"What happened after that?"

"I fled. Tripped over a body on my way out. I checked for a pulse and there was nothing. The kid was gone and then Maverick tackled me. The building blew and now you are caught up."

"You mentioned the DEA. Are you working with them as well, Ted?"

Thinking about my next reply carefully, I try to stall a bit.

"How's the new role treating you? You are a contractor now for different agencies, is that right?"

"Private investigator who occasionally assists other agencies. I know what you are trying to do. Stop stalling, Ted."

"I made a call to an old contact I had with the DEA. Hell, I wasn't even sure if the guy was still alive. Imagine my surprise when he answered the phone and knew who I was."

"What happened with that call?"

"I told him I would take him up on his offer now all these years later. He almost sounded relieved when I told him that. He mentioned that he had been observing me from afar for years but hadn't slipped up yet. He's been waiting a long time for that call from the sounds of it."

"Why now? What do they want, Ted?"

"They want the big fish. Whoever gives Stanley his orders and runs this whole thing."

"You don't know who that is?"

"This is a need-to-know kind of operation and all I need to know is my job and where I stand with the one directly above me which is Stanley. Anything else, is not my business."

"So, you've never been brought into the fold is what you are telling me?"

"That's exactly what I'm telling you. I'm also telling you that if I get them a name, they will reduce my sentence by half. The problem is getting the name before I get killed. I now have a Cartel guy who is off his rocker trying to kill everyone involved. And my old lieutenant is now out for my blood. Not to mention whoever oversees Stanley once they find out. I'm on the clock if you get my drift here."

"What about the kill order that's on us now?"

"Well, we killed Spencer, and I haven't seen Pierce since we were at the warehouse with the kid. So, unless someone else has brought new people into the fold, the kill order sits with me for now. But Paul, these recruits are like fucking cockroaches. You see one, and there's a bunch more hiding just out of sight."

He seems satisfied with the information I've given. He stands and stares at me for a minute before heading back into the office with Maverick and Fallon.

EMILY

Uncle Paul informs us of the conversation between him and Abbott.

"What he told Maverick is true. The Cartel likely blew up the building with some sort of incendiary device. I don't know why there was a second explosion. It could have been another device. Nothing else could have caused that much damage that quickly. That's for the local authorities to figure out. This specific Cartel is known for this. I also agree with Ted that Xander was working with someone else. My guess would be the DEA because this was essentially an elaborate drug operation. In a turn of events, the DEA reached out to Ted for his assistance in the same matter.

"Bullshit. You don't believe that do you?"

"I do, Emily. Remember how I told you that I had a few too many drinks when I told your dad about this operation with Abbott and Stanley?"

"Yes, but what does that have to do with anything?"

"Your dad went to the DEA with that information. He

took all the intel that you all found and had a contact within the organization. Someone he felt he could trust. I never got the name of his contact but Ted said that someone reached out to him ten years ago and wanted to make a deal. That he knew about your dad not being MIA but wanted Ted to help him bring the truth to light. Ted didn't want any part of that deal back then. He did manage to keep the number to that contact and made the call to move forward now with it. The man told Ted that he knew about Mike's disappearance and eventually death and that Ted had something to do with it. But they were willing to reduce his sentence because they want the big fish now. They want to shut this operation down once and for all and offered Ted a lighter sentence with his assistance. But he knows how this all works. You don't leave this organization any other way except for in a body bag or burial at sea."

"The agent offered him an out and witness protection but in order to get it, he needs the person pulling their strings. The problem is, even after all of these years, he's never been moved to the inner circle. He knows Stanley is up there, but he also knows someone pulls Stanley's strings. His objective was to find out who. He never told the DEA though that he would comply."

"Ted thinks that Xander was working with the DEA because of a potential safe word that he used right before things went sideways. He threw pineapple into a sentence which is something the DEA would have done. Something so obtuse so it wouldn't be misconstrued over a comm."

Pineapple? Why would that be Xander's safe word? I think to myself.

"So, why didn't the DEA bust in and take Xander out of there or Abbott for that matter?" Maverick asks.

"Maybe that was the other set of people that pulled up on the front side of the building that we heard, Mav."

"Ted said the room filled with smoke from smoke grenades. He thinks that was attributed from the DEA. He thinks they were there to get Xander out, but that they were too late to get to him and their focus changed to capturing the Cartel. Except my contacts say there has been chatter that the Cartel has already set off for home."

"Has anyone reached out to Abbott since this all went down?"

"Where is his phone?"

"On the table in the warehouse," says Maverick.

He walks out to grab the phone. When he comes back Mav tells us that there are six missed calls from an unknown number.

"If that phone rings again, answer it with Abbott at gunpoint. We need to know who is calling from that number," I order.

I look from my uncle to Mav and they silently agree.

"I hate to ask you this, Emily, but have you checked Xander's phone or laptop?"

"I don't have them. They were either with him or in his car. Is his car still here in Norfolk?"

"It is. We were a little preoccupied getting Abbott back here and of course you."

"We need those items I agree. How should we go about getting them?"

Abbott's phone begins to buzz from an incoming call from an unknown number.

"Take it to him to answer," I order.

Mav rushes out of the room with us right on his heels. He holds the phone and a gun to Abbott telling him to play along. The look on Abbott's face is annoyance but he plays along.

"What?" Abbott says after the phone is answered.

"Where are you?"

"I'm busy cleaning up this Cartel mess. What do you think I'm doing?"

"You are up to bat now, Abbott. Can you do this?"

I don't recognize the voice coming through the speaker. At first, I thought it was Stanley but there's a bit of an East Coast accent that Stanley does not have.

"You haven't given me much of a choice, have you? What do you need from me?"

"I told you we need the big fish, Abbott. Who is giving the orders to Stanley?"

"And I told you I don't know but I will find out. My terms still stand and I want it in writing."

"You will get it in writing. Now where's the kid?"

"Which kid? Pierce?"

"Don't play dumb with me. And no, we saw him get taken by the Cartel except he only made it to the trunk. They put a bullet in his head and shoved him inside."

I cover my mouth thinking about that being Xander and try to conceal my gasp.

"The Xander kid was still in the building last I saw him. I tried to protect him like you asked."

Abbott looks up at me when he says that last part. The part about trying to protect him.

"I was looking all over for him and even went back to get him but he wasn't at the table any longer. When I went toward the front to leave, I tripped over a body. His body."

I don't break eye contact and we are both too stubborn to back down.

"Shit. That's what we were afraid of."

With that comment, his fate is in fact sealed. He is gone and he was working with the DEA. Why didn't he think he could tell me? Why did he feel he had to hide this from us? From me? Anger starts to build and I leave the room and walk out the front door of the warehouse. I let out a scream that has been building inside me for the past few hours.

ABBOTT

"We will be in touch. Don't leave the state. And Abbott?"

"What?"

"Get us that name. You have twenty-four hours to comply, or the deal is off the table."

The call ends and Maverick puts the phone down.

"So, you are working with the DEA now? What's in it for you?" he asks me.

"Protection for people I care about. You heard him, I have twenty-four hours to get them a name or the deal is off. You have no reason to trust me and I get that but maybe after that call, we can agree to put our feelings aside to shut this down for good."

He turns to look at the door as his sister walks back in.

"Where are we?" she asks.

"They have given him twenty-four hours to provide the name of whoever is pulling Stanley's strings. We need him, Emme. We need to work with him to end this. For Xander."

Her cold dead eyes stare into me as she slowly nods in

agreement. I feel the hatred she has for me and I would expect nothing less.

"I will work with you because you tried to help Xander. For what purpose I don't know but because you tried, I won't drag out your death as I planned originally. We do this and then it's you and me Abbott."

She's got some massive Navy SEAL-size balls on her, I will give her that. In another life, she would have been a hell of an asset.

"We need a plan. I can get Stanley on the phone and even meet up with him but getting him to tell me, that's going to take a literal act of Congress. What's the plan?"

"You get him here, we will handle the rest," says Maverick.

"You are willing to take down an Admiral in the Navy, Maverick?"

"I'm willing to take the trash out of the military. He just happens to be an Admiral."

This whole family has some balls. I think to myself *that Mike Fallon would have been impressed.*

"I'll get him here. Call him."

Maverick grabs my phone and finds Stanley's number to call. He chuckles a little. I assume it's because I have him listed as Dick Stanley.

"Where the fuck have you been? What happened to the restaurant?" Is the "hello" we get from him.

"That's why I'm calling, you need to meet me. I'm sending you a pin. We need to pivot and quickly."

"I don't have time for this, orders have been given to take you out at first sight after this fuck up, Abbott."

"This isn't my fuck up, Robert. Your Cartel contact flipped the fuck out and pulled the literal trigger. He's the reason why the building blew. I also have it on good authority that Pierce was taken. Meet me so we can figure out how to get Gabriel what he wants and send him on his way. The kid already created the accounts but the numbers and the computer for that matter were in the building when it went."

"Send the pin and give me a few minutes to wrap some things up. The powers that be are pissed off and want heads to roll."

"Understandably, but it's their business partner that put this in motion. Maybe they should start there."

"Send the damn pin."

The call ends and Maverick shares our location with Stanley.

While we wait, I tell them that the tactics he used with me would work better on someone like Stanley. Skip the punching and jump straight to the battery and jumper cables. He might be an Admiral but he was put in that role, he didn't earn it. He's never fought for anything except more money.

Maverick nods in agreement.

"Fallon, you and Paul need to be out of sight. Well, all three of you until he gets inside this room. You will also need to free me from this chair. He will run like the coward he is if he sees that this is a trap."

Maverick takes a knife to cut the zip ties that keep my hands and feet strapped to the chair. I rub my wrists briefly.

"You might want to be facing the opposite direction when he walks in, your face is beaten to hell. He will likely flee if he sees you like this," says Paul.

A text comes through the phone from Stanley saying he will be here in ten minutes. We all look around the small warehouse to see if anything needs to be moved or put away before he arrives. Maverick moves the battery device and cables back to the table along the wall. He won't likely notice it right away.

Paul and Fallon move to the office location and Maverick stands inside the doorway with a gun aimed at me. I know he won't miss me if he takes a shot. The only thing keeping me going is knowing that the DEA has agreed to keep my family in Ecuador safe.

The door to the warehouse opens and Maverick steps back into the office a bit more to be out of Stanley's line of sight when he walks into the main room. I turn and start to walk to the opposite side trying to shield my face for a moment.

"Okay, I'm here. What's the plan? Tell me you have a plan, Ted."

"We need to find another place to clean the money. That's why Gabriel blew the building. He thought this was some sort of elaborate setup to catch him. He wasn't happy with the location and blew up the whole plan, literally."

I hear Stanley still moving forward so I start to turn toward him. Once I'm halfway around, I see that Maverick has moved behind him quietly to block his path if he were to attempt to escape.

"I tried to tell Gabriel that we could use the restaurant for storage and find a location that was ready to go."

"Gabriel do that to your face?"

"Something like that."

"What did you have in mind there, friend? My boss wants this wrapped up and it should have happened already."

"We've worked together long enough, Robert; I think you can finally tell me who your boss is."

"The less you know, my friend, the better off you are. Trust me on that."

"But I'm not, because Gabriel wants my head on a

platter and you threatened my family. So, who's it all for? Who has this much power over you if it isn't the Cartel. You owe me for all the shit I've done for you all these years."

"We will have to agree to disagree on this. You haven't been read in. You should be thankful for that."

Right then it clicks. I see a shift in his eyes and I know who's pulling his strings. The one that's been giving all the orders all these years.

"It's the Secretary of the motherfucking Navy, isn't it? That's the only person that makes any sense. She's been giving you orders for years. Providing reasons to other Admirals as to why you needed to be on certain deployments. I can't believe that I missed that all this time. You and Jack have been friends for ages. How did I miss this?"

"I told you friend; this goes way beyond us. This isn't personal." He goes for his weapon.

Maverick grabs him and disarms him from behind.

"Nice try there, Admiral, but we still need him for a bit longer," Maverick tells him.

"You are working with the Fallons, now? Your family made you soft didn't they, Ted? This is the choice you made then? I'm sure Maria and Miggy will understand. I'll make sure they are taken out quietly."

"Fuck you. You put us all in an impossible situation by making us SECNAV's bitch. That's why people conveniently disappear while out to sea or are dismissed from the Navy without reasons given. None need to be given when it's the Secretary of the fucking Navy giving the damn order."

Stanley stands there quietly for a moment.

Emily comes through the office and stands directly in front of Stanley.

"Who made the call to kill our father and David?"

"I did. To protect the operation."

Well, that was dumb on his part. I don't think he was aware that she is at a brand-new level of anger right now or he wouldn't have answered that so quickly. She sweeps his legs out from under him forcing him to land on his back. She steps on his throat cutting off his airway. As he attempts to struggle against her, she hits him in the jugular then leans down to grab him by his collar and slams his head into the concrete floor.

"Emily, stop! We need him right now," Paul yells at her.

Maverick pulls her off of him and tries to restrain her a bit.

Maverick orders Paul and Fallon to go get Xander's car. He's hoping the laptop is in there and maybe that will provide some answers. She pushes past Maverick with Paul right behind her as they leave the building.

For now, Maverick, Robert and I wait and figure out what our next move should be as the clock continues its countdown.

EMILY

My uncle drives us in his vehicle because mine and Maverick's are still at the location down the street from where Xander last was. It takes us a little bit to get there but when we do, I immediately exit the car. The car is parked a few blocks away from mine and Maverick's vehicles.

The emotions start to churn inside me, but I need to see if anything is left in his car that we can use. I try the door. It opens right up. That's odd. He always locks his doors. Almost to the point of annoying. He even locks them when his car is parked in the garage. Maybe Abbott's story pans out about him being taken.

After I climb into the driver's seat, I take a deep breath. Everything smells like him. His woodsy clean smell lingers in the air. He was in this car a few hours ago. This still doesn't seem real. I slam my hands on the steering wheel wanting it to fight back.

I know I need to pull myself together. Looking around the car, I see that in the passenger seat is his work backpack. I grab it, open it, and see his laptop, some snacks, an envelope, and his phone are all placed inside. I turn in the seat to see if there is anything else I should grab. His car is meticulously clean. Feeling my eyes fill with tears, I blink quickly trying to not let them fall. A few deep breaths help to keep them in check. Looking around one more time, nothing stands out, so I take the bag back to my uncle's car and we head back to the warehouse.

* * *

Once I'm back in my uncle's car, I open the envelope first to find a typed note.

Xander, you don't know me, but I have intel on Mike's murder. Check your email for more information. Don't tell anyone.

Mike? My dad? Who sent this to him? When was this sent to him? A whole new set of questions come rushing into my mind. The letter said to check his email.

"Have you seen this before?" I hand my uncle the note.

He takes the typed piece of paper and looks at it as if it's the first time he's seen it. I believe the expression on his face is truthful.

"No, this is the first time I've seen this, Emily."

"Who sent this to him? Why didn't he tell me or us?"

"He was probably looking into it first before bringing it to the rest of us."

"He wouldn't do that, though."

"But he did, Emily."

Next, I open up the laptop. I'm greeted with a password. What are the chances it's something I would know? Trying the first two things that come to mind, my birth date and the day we met, neither of which are correct. Xander is… was a very analytical person and great with numbers. I try the same dates but in reverse order. That's it! It was my birth date but typed backwards.

Once I'm in, I go to his email to see what messages he's been receiving or sending lately. Most are boring work emails for his contracting company but two in his deleted folder grab my attention. They are from someone named Keith. Keith says he knew my father and he wanted Xander to meet him. Is this who is behind all of this? Does this Keith person work for the DEA?

"Do you know a Keith?"

"I can't say that I do, Emily, why do you ask?"

"Someone named Keith emailed Xander a few days back. Twice actually, the second email basically explains how he got Xander's information. Do you think this was one of the DEA people reaching out to him?"

"If I ventured a guess, I would say yes but we don't have a way to prove that."

"You have so many contacts. Can't you call one of them?" I yell.

"Emily, it doesn't work like that with what I do. I have as many people looking into this as I can."

For the remainder of the trip, we are silent.

* * *

We get back to the warehouse and not much has changed. Abbott, Stanley, and Maverick are in the same space we left them in. They are arguing about something but get quiet when we enter the room.

"Where are you with a plan, Maverick?" I ask.

"At this point, we have the name and can provide that for leverage as needed to the DEA."

"What were you all arguing about?"

"These two idiots think they can take SECNAV out. I've

tried to explain that it will need to be a long game type of plan. She's very smart, but we are smarter."

"Agreed we need to think of a plan but first, do either of you know a Keith?" I ask to Stanley and Abbott.

"That's my DEA contact. Why?"

"He was also Xander's."

"Why are you asking, Fallon?" inquires Abbott.

"I found a note and a few emails from Keith saying that he knew our dad, had some information about him and wanted to meet with Xander."

"He was his handler, Fallon, but that's all I know. He kept us separate until the warehouse."

Shifting back to the information that we were discussing earlier. "Has anyone stopped to wonder why Stanley was so willing to give up the name?" I ask to nobody in particular.

"I'm dead regardless of me giving you the name. Anyone that works for the devil is going to get burned and frankly, I'm exhausted and want this to end as much as you do. She's had a power hold over me for years. Even before the trips to Ecuador started."

Once I'm satisfied with his reply I ask the room, "How are we taking this bitch down?"

ABBOTT

"Stanley and I know how these people work. If you will let us help you, maybe we can end this once and for all."

"Are you kidding, Abbott? He just told us the Secretary of the Navy is the fucking ringleader. It might as well be the President of the United States. We are as good as dead," she says with disdain.

"I didn't say it would be easy but it isn't impossible."

She looks at me, at Maverick, Paul, and finally Stanley.

"What's your plan?"

"Robert, do you have any information like files, photos, emails or anything that would help us end this?"

"I've been saving some things for years. A recorded conversation that I had with the Secretary. After I told her about Mike and how we handled it, I got her on a recording saying to keep it between us but that she was happy to know that I was willing to do what it takes for EM-Comm. That's how she refers to this whole operation, as EM-Comm, Ecuador Movement Command.

"I have one more recording that was before she was

appointed to her current role. Looking back now, I'm so glad I thought to record these conversations. I never thought I would need them. Jack and I go way back. We came up through the Navy together. With all my indiscretions, I was halted in any forward progress. She found someone to shoot her to the top though. No matter the cost. The only reason I haven't been dishonorably discharged is because of her. She's covered for me more than once. The two of those together should be worth something don't you think?"

Fallon and her brother look like they want to tear Robert limb from limb.

"You will get your turn, Fallon. I see that look in your eyes and know what you feel right now. But you need to reign it the fuck in."

Maverick steps in front of me. Nose to nose and says, "Don't talk to her like that."

"Maverick it's fine. I can handle myself. And when this is all over, you both will get what's coming to you. I will make sure of it if it's the last thing I do."

Directing my attention back to Robert, I ask, "Where are these recordings?"

"At my home in Duck."

"We need to get those recordings," I tell the Fallons. "Once we have those in our possession we can move on to the next step."

"Which is?" Maverick inquires.

"Taking down SECNAV."

"How do you suppose that we do that?" Paul chimes in.

"We need to build a case against her. The recordings will help and any other info that you can provide to us, Robert."

"I'll see what I can come up with."

Robert continues, "I was simply a pawn accepting the

risk in the Queen's game. Be careful how you proceed. She is smart and has people everywhere reporting back to her. I'm sure she knows I'm here. I truly believe my demise is only a matter of time. Taking the Queen down is like cutting the head off a very powerful snake."

"I thought you were the rook like the one you carry around with you," I question.

"Right now, I'm the pawn. Remember that if things were to go south, Abbott."

Looking toward the Fallons, I tell them, "We need those recordings." I direct my attention back to Robert. "Do you have anything else we can use on her?"

"I might but you will need to dig into it to make sure all the dots connect before using the information."

"What is it?" I ask him,

"It's my understanding that she wasn't the first choice for her role. The president had another person in mind. He was persuaded a bit to put her there."

"What proof do you have for this?" Maverick asks him.

"Originally, I was sent an anonymous tip. Someone sent me photos of the President having several interactions with a gentleman that he wanted for that role. It was public knowledge that he intended to appoint Mitchell Thomas. He was a prominent naval strategist."

"Was?" I goad.

"I'll get to that. The meetings that he had with Mitchell were all above board. Someone who works with him very closely confirmed that he has never had a meeting with Jack. Not one. I honestly don't believe that he had anything to do with what I'm about to tell you."

Stanley looks to all of us before continuing. After a moment of silence, he goes on.

"Mitchell was found dead in his home three weeks before Jack's appointment was announced. The Senate called a meeting with the POTUS and a new plan was formed."

"She has standing meetings every Wednesday with some of the President's advisors and members of the Senate. The very same ones that I feel swayed his vote in her direction. From those meetings, she's made some interesting calls."

"What are you suggesting, Robert?"

"That she was put in that role for the wrong reasons. I think she has leverage on some very powerful people in Washington. She put herself in that office, a position of power. If we can prove that and add in the recordings, we can end all of this. Taking out the entire EM-Comm organization."

"That's a tall order, friend. How do we prove this?"

"I scanned the original photos and put them on one of the drives with one of the recordings, but for the other items, you will have to figure out how to connect them back."

"Sorry to interrupt, but our priority right now is to get the target off our backs. We need leverage. Let's start with the recordings and we will work on everything else," Fallon interjects.

"We need to get our ears into one of those meetings," Paul suggests.

"How would you like us to go about doing that?" Maverick asks.

"The one person capable of doing that is now gone. He taught Mav and I some things but I'm not confident we can set it up without leaving a digital footprint on her PC."

"You have very little time to figure this out. Robert, you are up. Get back to your house tonight and we will come to you once we wrap up things here and listen to the recordings. Paul and I will go back to his place and figure out where we go from here."

"What about the targets on all of us?" Maverick asks.

"We won't be leaving this site. Both Emily's place and mine have been compromised. It is safer staying here for now," Paul advises.

"Stay alert, don't draw attention to yourselves, and watch each other's backs. That's all I have right now. I don't know who she will send to replace Pierce, Spencer, and eventually me once she gets word that I'm now working with Team Fallon."

"Another question, she has tons of security right now, how do you expect us to get into her office at some point?" Fallon asks.

"Robert, can you be her detail for one meeting and maybe a few people that you trust to appoint? Somehow get her away from her office for maybe thirty minutes?"

"It's a possibility. I've been asked to work on her detail before. But I also know she can lose them when it's needed. I've been advised to never ask her to do that unless it's a matter of national security."

"Make this be a national security item, Robert. That you will be her security for a meeting with the Cartel. If she's running this whole thing, maybe that will be enough to get her to leave."

We talk over the next few hours to nail out a plan. The Fallons agree to let Robert go back to his house to start the process of contacting SECNAV. The Fallons do not agree to let me leave as I figured.

EMILY

*M*averick and I clean up the warehouse while Uncle Paul and Abbott continue to talk through the plan. His main objective right now is to keep Abbott out of sight. It's close to midnight and my mind races to the fact that Xander is still gone. The guys all offer me the couch to get some sleep while they continue to clean up and get us ready to head over to Stanley's house. There is no way that I can sleep right now. My mind won't stop replaying the explosion. It's like an old VHS tape that is stuck in one spot on one image. Only this image plays over and over again in my mind and I can't seem to make it stop.

It's nearing 1:00 a.m. Maverick goes around the warehouse making sure all the windows and doors are still in place and locked. I'm hugging Xander's PC and I don't even realize it until I walk over to the couch to try and get some sleep.

"Did you have a chance to look at his PC, Emme?" he asks.

"I did briefly while we were heading back here from

Norfolk. I found two emails from a Keith asking him to meet. Something about our dad? Do you know a Keith?"

"No, I don't. Abbott said he was Xander's handler and his. At one point he was also dad's. Dad never mentioned him to me. I'm surprised like you are, Emme. Did you find anything else?"

"That's all I had time for before we got back to the warehouse."

"Mind if I take a look before we leave?"

"That's fine, I'll leave it here on the desk for you."

Maverick walks over to me and embraces me in a hug. He pulls back and smooths the hair away from my face.

"Emme, you don't have to be this strong. I know you need to grieve and that's okay. I'm here for you as a shoulder to cry on, punch, kick, or whatever it is you need to do. But you need to feel this before it consumes you."

My shoulders drop slightly because I feel the weight of everything. I straighten them and respond to him without the filter I had been using.

"Maverick, I hear what you are saying and I will take the time to do all of those things once this shit with SECNAV is behind us. I want that bitch's head on a fucking platter."

"Think about what I said. If at any time this becomes too much, all of us understand."

"Mav, I love you, but this whole thing with the EM-Comm ends now. I'm taking anyone and everyone out that's affiliated with it one by one, leaving scorched earth and bodies in my wake."

He nods and I can see that he's worried about me, especially after my last remark but now is my time to rise up and fight for everyone that is no longer here to fight for themselves. I carry their voices inside me. So many untold stories and experiences that they won't ever experience because their lives were extinguished too soon. My determination and unwavering resolve to honor the memories of our dearly departed is palpable. I internally enlist myself as the guardian of their legacy.

Heading over to the couch, I turn and tell Maverick I need to wash up.

"There's a small bathroom on the other side of the empty room. When you are done, please try to get a few hours' sleep. We will be leaving soon but until then, try to rest. I have a feeling it's going to be a long day."

I nod and walk out of the small office to clean up a bit. The adrenaline from today and the warm water from washing my face makes me sleepy and my body agrees to stop fighting the sleep that inevitably will take over.

* * *

I jump up to my phone sounding an alert. It isn't 6:00 a.m. yet so it isn't my alarm. Reaching for it in the still-dark room, I see that someone sent me an email. Clicking into it, my breath catches, and my heart literally skips a beat.

Ems, if you are reading this, things didn't go as planned. I can't tell you what happened exactly, but I can tell you that I did what I needed to do to protect you. A few days back a man named Keith started to reach out. First by a letter left on our doorstep and then by email. He was adamant that he knew your dad and had additional info. Going against my better judgement, I agreed to meet him. He told me that I needed to help him to keep you safe and out of prison. It was a no-brainer my love. I would walk to the ends of the earth for you. The plan was simple. I was to set up some accounts for a client and in return, you would stay out

of prison. He had some pretty damning evidence against you.

I didn't lie about having to go to Norfolk but I'm sure you know about that by now. This email was scheduled to send to you, the only way to stop it was if I were alive. I'm so sorry we won't have our wedding day but I didn't need a special day to tell you how much I love you and how I would never have left you willingly. You are probably cussing me out and I don't blame you but know that my heart was in the right place, where it always is, with you. I wish we would have had the chance to dance to our song.

I will love you always and have loved you forever.
Love,
Xander

My heart breaks into a million pieces all over again. Literally shattered every bit that was left with that email. I look at the timestamp and it was sent a few moments ago. Jumping up I yell for Maverick who's asleep in one of the chairs across from me.

"What? What is it, Emme?"

"Where's the laptop?"

"It's here on the floor next to me. What's wrong?"

"Xander emailed me."

"Emme, that's impossible."

"I know. I know I sound crazy but here, look for yourself."

I toss him my phone with the email still pulled up on the screen. He's silent as he reads it. Placing a hand over his mouth to cover the shocked look, he looks at me with pure surprise.

"How did he send this to you?"

"I'm sure it was set to be a delayed delivery. I need to

see his computer to see if I can find out more information about it."

He hands it over and then joins me on the couch while I check the email.

I quickly access his email and do a trace. It provides info reflecting that the email was sent on a delay and received by me. Also, the sender was in fact Xander. The metadata also reflects that the message was scheduled midmorning yesterday. Likely before he left to get our rings and drive to Norfolk. All the things I hoped for weren't the case. I close his laptop and head out into the empty room beyond the office door. Maverick follows right behind me.

"Emme, you okay?"

"I'll be okay once this is over. I'm going to freshen up and then we can head to Stanley's to get started on our plan."

"Sounds good. I'll try to find us some quick breakfast while you get ready."

"Thank you for being here, Mav. It means everything to me."

"Little sister, I wouldn't have it any other way."

I leave the office to get ready for our day. On my way to the bathroom, I hear a reporter talking about the explosion from Maverick's phone. This is going to be my life for the next several months I'm sure.

Fifteen minutes later as I'm gathering my things that might be needed today, I hear Maverick yell to me.

"Emme, you about ready to go? It's time to head to Stanley's place. Everything here is locked up, cleaned up or going with us. Here's some food for you to eat on the way. It isn't much but should take the edge off a bit."

"I'm almost ready," I holler back while tucking my gun into my waistband.

ABBOTT

"We've been over this and over this, Paul. We need those USB drives and the Fallons to get into her office. That's it. Robert gets her away from her office, they get in there and plant whatever it is they plan to use on her PC."

"Lower your voice please. I think Emily is finally getting some rest. I'm fine sticking to the plan."

The Fallons walk into the room Paul and I are in.

"It's just us," says Maverick.

"Emme and I were talking, we think we should head over now to Stanley's place to get the drives. There's no point in waiting. We have done all we can do here for now. The longer we wait, the better chance we have of being found by one of SECNAV's low life scum."

"Your uncle mentioned the same thing. If everyone is fine with that, let's go. We should take one car though. The neighborhood he lives in will notice two cars that don't belong there. Assuming the neighbors are awake this early."

With that, we all head out to the parking lot, climb into Paul's vehicle, and head toward Duck, NC.

* * *

Within ten minutes we approach his house. The look on the Fallon's faces is in awe of what we they are seeing. The architectural elegance and timeless charm of his home stand out against the others in this area. The wrought iron fencing adorned with intricate scrollwork stretches down the entire property line. Some would wonder what secrets are being guarded within the property.

"Looks like the drug business pays exceptionally well because he did not get this house off his Admiral salary alone," Maverick points out as we drive up the brick-laid drive that circles all the way to the back of the house. Each brick is a testament to the craftsmanship used to create this masterpiece. We can see an inground pool and hot tub as we pass the front of the home that is meticulously cared for. The smell of lavender and freshly mowed lawns linger in the air, creating an atmosphere of serenity and grace.

Circling around back, I notice the ivy-covered walls that hold stories of countless gatherings and whispered conversations. If these walls could talk, we wouldn't need to be here.

"Does Stanley have a large family?" Fallon asks from the back seat.

"The exact opposite. This is for him and him alone. He's spent lots of money making this house into a private oasis for himself."

Paul parks the car and we all ascend up the brick stairs onto the wrap-around porch. I turn the doorknob to check to see if it's locked before knocking. It opens right up.

"Robert, we couldn't sleep so we came over to get this started," I holler through the house.

No response.

"He's probably asleep. Wait here and I will go get him," I say as I jog up the curved carpeted staircase that leads up to the bedrooms.

"Robert? You up here?" I check his room and the bed is still made so if he is here, he's somewhere else in the house. I yell down the stairs to have them split up and look for him and maybe not touch anything just to be safe. Continuing my search of the upstairs room results in nothing.

"Anyone have anything?" I ask the other three.

"Nothing from me. The downstairs is clear, but I do have a bit of envy over his game room," Maverick jokes.

"The main level is clear as well. But seriously why does one person need this much space?" Fallon replies.

As I join them on the main level, I see the Fallon's faces etched with concern. I can sense their anxiety with each passing moment. We've scoured every room of the house. The interior of the home is perfectly decorated with antique furniture and dimly lit chandeliers, making it feel both eerie and unfamiliar. The house is silent. I fear the worst.

"Everyone I found him. He's in the garage. Make sure you don't touch anything and if you touched something already, go clean it. Now!" Paul orders.

We all move slowly to the interior garage door. Under a single bulb that is casting long shadows, we see Robert sitting in his car. In front of the interior door are some towels to help contain the fumes from the car that likely ran all night. Robert's lifeless form is slumped in the driver's seat. His private oasis is now his tomb. A reminder that some of the darkest secrets are hidden in the most unexpected places.

"He was right, they knew he talked to us," Fallon tells us.

"We need to look for those USB Drives. Don't touch anything without cleaning up after yourself. Let's split up," I tell them.

Paul interjects, "Wait. Before we start looking through the entire house, what were his exact words about SECNAV? Anyone remember? He mentioned something about him being a pawn. How did he phrase it?"

"Why is this relevant right now? We found his dead body in his car and we all look suspicious, we need to leave, not decode prior conversations."

"Emily, I'm serious. Robert was a huge chess player."

"Paul's right. For as long as I've known him, he's always carried around this rook chess piece. One time I asked him about it and he said it was a reminder for him about his place in the world."

"Maverick, you mentioned you were envious of his game room. I know for a fact that his pride and joy is in that room. It's this hand-carved board and hand-carved pieces that he had specifically made for himself. I had to hear about it all the damn time when we traveled. He was the one to teach me how to play chess. Please work with me here and help me remember what he said. I think that might have something to do with the drive's location," Paul informs the room.

We all look at Paul like he might be crazy, but I also think he might be onto something. Robert would be someone who would hide something like this in plain sight. We all walk back into the main house and head down to the game room. The dark wood paneling and lack of windows, make it feel like it's much later than it is when in this room.

In the center of the room, almost as if it were on

display, sits two very solid, leather, tufted back cushions, and nail head trim armchairs with wooden legs. Between the two chairs is a wooden raised table with his handcrafted chess board set for a new game.

"Does anyone other than Uncle Paul know how to play chess?" asks Maverick.

"We don't need to play, but what did he say about the Queen? I think he was telling us where the drives are. If I'm right, this board has everything to do with it."

Paul walks around the board eying it carefully. "This board looks like it would have a drawer on it doesn't it?" he asks nobody in particular.

"It does look raised or maybe something opens on it to hold the pieces?" Fallon suggests.

"No, the pieces came in a separate wooden case that was also handcrafted. Robert loved chess. His first real expense to himself other than fixing up this house, was this board and the pieces to it."

"I've been thinking about his comment and I think he said that he was a pawn and the Queen assumes the risk," Fallon interjects.

"No that doesn't make sense, but if you turn it around and say it, it's actually a well-known chess move," Paul corrects.

He looks around the room briefly and walks over to the bar area to grab something. He comes back to the chess set with a napkin and starts to tell us what he remembers, "Robert said that he was simply a pawn accepting the risk in the Queen's game. He was telling us about the game he loved. He was telling us a move. It's called the Queen's Gambit. It's one of the oldest moves in chess. It allows you to have control of the middle of the board. Look at this board, the squares all look like puzzle pieces. They fit perfectly together but also can't come apart. Most chess boards are one solid piece. I say we try the move," Paul suggests.

We all look at Paul and agree. He takes the napkin and begins to demonstrate the move.

"The move is rather simple, really. White would start by moving the queen's pawn two spaces to D4. Black will likely counter and do the same, moving their queen's pawn two spaces to D5. The last move is white moving their queen's side bishop pawn forward two squares to C4."

We are all staring at the board wondering what will happen once the move is completed. Paul moves the last piece into place, but nothing happens.

"Are you sure that's how the move works?" Maverick questions.

"Let me start over, maybe I'm missing something."

Paul moves the pieces to their starting positions. As he places one of the pieces back to its original location, the look on his face shifts to a perplexed one.

"What is it, Paul?"

"When I moved this piece back, it felt almost like a magnet. Like there's a pull to it."

I walk over to the bar to grab another napkin to see what he's talking about. Lifting the same piece, I try to move it.

"It's magnetic," I agree with him.

"What if you slide the pieces while recreating the move?" Fallon suggests.

"That's a brilliant idea, Emily," Paul states as he restarts the Queen's Gambit.

He slides the first piece to D4. You can hear an audible shift of metal. He looks up at us to make sure we all heard the same thing.

I drag the opponent's piece to D5. A clicking occurs below the surface of the board, but nothing on the surface has happened. The final move is to C4. Paul looks at each of us as he slides the queen bishop's pawn to C4. The four of us are on pins and needles wondering what's about to happen.

He completes the move by sliding the final piece into place.

There is an audible unlocking sound. Paul lets out a breath then says, "The point of the move is to gain control of the center of the board."

The center of the board is raised slightly, Paul takes the napkin to encourage it out of its spot. Inside one of the squares is a foam insert holding two USB drives.

"Okay, we need to put everything back the way it was and get the hell out of here," I order them.

EMILY

We leave Stanley's house in Duck, NC, a little after 7:30 a.m. hoping that we didn't leave anything that would link any of us there. Getting back to the warehouse we gather around the desk in the office area to see what's on these drives. Maverick plugs the first one in. It tells us there is only one audio file. The rest of the device is blank.

"Sorry, but before we listen to these don't you think we should report that Stanley was murdered or call the cops?" I ask to the room.

"Trust me, Fallon, someone will find him soon enough," replies Abbott.

Maverick selects the file. It takes a bit to load but once it does, he turns up the speaker on the PC to hear the recording. It's a bit muffled but you can get the gist of what's being said.

"What did you need to speak to me about so urgently, Robert?"

There's a pause. Maverick checks to make sure it hasn't

stopped recording. He gives us a thumbs-up as someone begins to talk again.

"Stop pacing. You are making me anxious. Tell me what is so important that you had me cancel my meeting."

"On the last trip to Ecuador, Mike Fallon kept sticking his nose into our business. He was onto us. He even provided some information to the DEA we think. I can't prove that last part, but he knew about our operation and the DEA had been asking around about the ship and it's intended target."

"And was Mike handled?"

"He was. I had Abbott take care of him."

My fists at my sides keep flexing while I try not to go after Abbott hearing that comment.

The recording continues.

"It's good to know that you are willing to do what it takes to protect EM-Comm. I knew I made the right choice with you, Robert. Is that all?"

"You aren't mad?"

"Why would I be? You knew there was an issue and you handled it before it went further."

There's another pause in the recording. Maverick removes the drive and inserts the next one.

"That was what he was talking about with your dad. I think that recording will be helpful. But, Ted, it incriminates you as well," explains Uncle Paul.

"I don't care, I knew one way or another I would be paying for the crimes I've committed."

"We ready to see what's on the other one?" Maverick asks.

He inserts the next one and again, one audio file but also the scanned images Stanley told us about. All of POTUS and we assume Mitchell Thomas.

Once he confirms we are good to go, he hits play.

"Come in." You hear in the distance.

"Captain Cohen, do you have a moment?"

"What the hell are you doing standing in the doorway of my office, Lieutenant Stanley?"

"That's why I'm here, Ma'am. I wish I could explain what happened but I can't. My memory is completely blank about the events from last night, but what I know is that I missed my ship. I'm hoping that confronting this now is some sort of saving grace. You must know it wasn't deliberate, Jack."

"Don't call me that, Lieutenant. We might go back a long time, but at this station and in this room, I am your superior. You will address me accordingly."

"Yes ma'am. Sorry ma'am"

"What happened?"

"From what I remember, some guys from my unit and I went out to celebrate before having to leave this morning. I remember starting at some hole-in-the-wall place and then moving on to another. I don't remember much after that. Then this morning, I woke up to basically a vacant apartment. I was alone and my car was parked in an alley outside the apartment.

Sitting here listening to these recordings my thoughts are a whirlwind of confusion and suspicion. "It sounds like he was drugged. Do you all agree?" I ask looking around the room to Maverick, Abbott, and Uncle Paul.

They shrug but seem to agree with me.

The recording continues. My brow furrows with concern as I continue to listen.

"Have you reached out to the other people in your unit to see if they can provide some insight to your evening, Lieutenant?"

"No, because they are on my ship. My Commanding officer called a few times and left me a voicemail. He is also on my ship and I'm sure it's been noticed that I am not. I wanted to speak with you first."

"Have you been checked out by medical yet?"

"No, you were my first stop."

"We have a situation here, that's for sure. You realize you missing ships movement is grounds for dismissal?"

"I'm aware, but I'm hoping there is something that can be done. This is an unusual situation. You know I would have been on that ship any other way."

"This is your third offense, Lieutenant; your time here is done. First, you had a failure to adhere to the Navy uniform regulations because you continually were caught not properly maintaining your uniform components."

"I don't know what happened to my items. They kept disappearing. I know that isn't a good reason, but I can't explain what happened to them."

"Your uniforms and the components are your responsibility, Lieutenant. The only person to blame is yourself."

"Don't forget about the unauthorized equipment modification for trying to alter some of the naval hardware without proper approval."

"That was my misunderstanding. I thought you had already cleared it. I took full responsibility for that one."

"As you should have, Lieutenant. I was still in the process of getting authorization when you decided to do the modifications."

"There must be something you can do. I came here because of our history and because you're my friend, not because you are my superior. I know you have a job to do but I was looking for your guidance. This is me begging you, Jack."

"I said to not call me that. Let me think."

There is another brief pause in the recording. Mav gives us another thumbs up to let us know that it's still playing.

"There might be something I can do. First, you need to get cleared by medical and they need to put it in your medical chart that you lost consciousness. That will give you a few days here at the station."

"Then what?"

"I'm getting to that. You will be assigned to the USS Harrison."

"Why the USS Harrison?"

"It's our ship that goes to Ecuador for the Naval exercises with other countries. You will be on a specific assignment each time it's sent out. What I'm about to tell you is not to leave this room. You utter anything about this, I will have you court marshaled so fast your fucking head will spin. Do you hear me?"

"Loud and clear, ma'am."

"There is an organization that I oversee that handles covert operations. A clandestine network designed to facilitate a seamless exchange of classified information. We have a contact in Ecuador that you will meet with each time you are sent out. Your duties will include giving the Mayor of Manta a tour of our ship, overseeing drills between the different Navies, and meeting with this contact."

A chilling realization creeps over me. "She set this whole thing in motion. She probably even had him drugged so he didn't have another option or way out."

"I think you are exactly right, Emily. This was her plan all along. She probably was responsible for his other indiscretions as well."

We go back to listening to the recording.

"Why am I meeting with this person?"

"I'm getting to that. You will provide him with the coordinates for our ships and the others that are down there for the week."

"Why would I do that, ma'am?"

"Do you know what's been happening around the ports in Ecuador?"

"I know other countries try to smuggle drugs in and around their ports."

"Providing the coordinates to the contact allows him to give

that to the Cartel. They will use that to avoid being caught by us or any of the other countries that are protecting the ports."

"I see."

"Is this a problem for you, Robert?"

"Now we are using first names, Jack?"

"Listen to me very carefully. You will navigate this task each time with precision and subtlety. If you can't do this, then we can proceed with your court marshal. You like chess, right?"

"Yes, what does chess have to do with this?"

"Because this is your only move. You got yourself backed into a corner. But if you agree to this new role, you will be paid handsomely after each trip. At some point, you will need to find a few trustworthy people to work with you. I've noticed you and Ted Abbott are pretty close. Maybe read him in but keep him at an arm's length. There will be times when you won't be available to meet our contact or one of his men. We don't want to miss that appointment. All of our asses are on the line here."

"Who's been handling this up until now?"

"Nobody. It has been in the works for some time but this week the first meeting happens. You represent me when you meet him."

"How do I contact this person?"

There is some rustling in the background.

"This phone has one number in it. The contact. When he messages, you make yourself available and meet him at the location that he will send to you. You have thirty minutes to get to the meet site."

"And if I can't make it in thirty minutes."

"You don't want to find out what happens so don't be late."

"Robert, can you do this?"

"What other options do I have right now, Jack?"

"None, but once this starts, there is only one way out and nobody will know what happened to you. Am I making myself clear?"

"I understand."

"Go see medical and let me know today what they say."
"Robert?"
"Yes ma'am?"
"Welcome to EM-Comm."

After that last comment, there is a long section of silence and then nothing else.

Maverick stops the recording and we all look at one another.

"She has had this whole thing planned from day one. She's the ringleader in all of this. All the pieces are starting to fall into place. And now it's time for her to be taken down," I explain. "When did Stanley bring you into the fold, Abbott?"

"About twelve years ago. He had a pretty good system in place for those trips so this recording was more than twelve years old. He's been holding this for a long time."

"Ted, you need to call your DEA contact, this information is exactly what they need to take her down."

"Bullshit! They are not ending this, I am!"

My determination to uncover the truth surges through me. It's going to be a race against time to untangle the web of deceit in order to prove her involvement in this.

"Emme, you need to let them handle this. Someone as high up as her, she needs to be handled correctly or it will all be for nothing."

"Or what, Mav, she will come after me? Let her fucking come because I will be waiting."

ABBOTT

*A*s Maverick and Fallon go back and forth, I walk into the other room and call my contact.

"Hey, we have something and I have a name. But you need to come to us for the info."

"Where are you?"

"I'll drop a pin from my burner. And bring my written agreement because you aren't getting shit until I see it in person."

"I already picked it up. I'll head your way as soon as you send your location."

Hanging up the call, I walk back into the office.

"DEA is on the way. We ready for this? Once they get involved it will all move fast."

"Or we will all get killed like Xander did," Fallon comments dryly.

We sit in silence until we hear a car pull into the parking lot twenty minutes later. We all focus on the front door waiting to see who walks in. I see that it's my guy. He still looks like he did all those years ago, just a little more gray in his hair. I meet him at the door and let him in, leading him to the office.

"Everyone this is Keith, he's with the DEA and he's going to help us."

Fallon shoots out of her chair but Maverick grabs her around the waist before she can get too far.

"Thanks, Maverick," I tell him.

"You got Xander killed, you asshole. How can you stand there and pretend to not know who we are."

"I know exactly who you are, Emily Renee Fallon. Xander did what he did to protect you. He was trying to keep you safe while helping his country."

"By having him lie to me?"

"The less you knew the better."

"We could have helped him. Do you not get that? He would still be here, but you didn't give us that opportunity and now because of you, he's gone."

"I understand you are upset. Nobody wanted him to get hurt, Emily. We took precautions to keep him safe. I couldn't risk any leaks, not even to you. We didn't know that Gabriel would show up with equipment to blow a damn building. Nobody could have known that."

Xander being taken from her while he was trying to protect her is a tragedy. His mission was shrouded in secrecy and Keith was the agent responsible for that.

She walks off to another room and Maverick follows her.

"Where's my written agreement?"

"Right here, look it over, and then sign it. We will talk after you do that."

He hands me a document that's a couple of pages. I read through it carefully. It says everything we agreed to. "What happens after I sign this?" I ask.

"We take you in and start working on shutting the person down from the name you give me."

The forms state that if I give the name and any additional information that I might come across, in return, I will go to prison but at a reduced sentence for cooperating. Doesn't matter really. SECNAV has people everywhere, if she wants me dead, she will make a call and have it done.

"Gotta pen?"

Keith hands me a pen and I sign the form. "Let's talk about something we discovered this morning. First, you need to alert someone that Robert Stanley is dead. He's in his garage at his home in Duck. It was set up to look like a suicide but everyone in here knows that isn't the case."

"How do you know this, Abbott?" Keith questions.

"We planned to meet him this morning, but he didn't answer the door so we checked the house and that's when we found him. Don't worry we were thorough before we left and wiped any of our prints off any of the surfaces we might have touched."

"Let me make a call, I'll be back."

Keith walks outside for a few minutes.

"Where's he going?" asks Emily as she and Maverick rejoin us.

"I told him about Robert so he's calling it in."

Keith walks back into the room. "I called it in, but the housekeeper found him a little after she got there this morning. It's currently being ruled as a suicide. We will have someone from our team reach out and check on the case. It's time to get down to business. What do you have, Abbott?"

I hold out my hand to encourage him to have a seat at the dining room table. After he takes a seat we all join him and I start first.

"Yesterday I had the opportunity to speak with Robert

with these people as witnesses. They can corroborate the info I'm about to tell you."

"Continue."

"Robert confirmed that the Secretary of the Navy is in charge of something called EM-Comm." I let that sit with him for a moment. He looks at me like he's waiting for me to give him the punchline.

"You serious?"

"Yes. I am. Robert was able to provide us with two recordings. One has her making him a patsy in her whole plan. He's been her go-to person for years. We all listened to the recordings and think she had him drugged one night. He lost his memory from it and missed his ship's movement the following day. He was already on thin ice. She basically dangled one option in front of him. That option was to be her contact with the Cartel. He was the initial contact. Once he had it down, he was allowed to bring others in. I came in a few years later."

"You realize that you are accusing the Secretary of the United States Navy of espionage, drug smuggling, treason, and about five other crimes? Someone who is entrusted with upholding the law and protecting our nation's interests. You are telling me that she forged an alliance with a Cartel to leverage their knowledge of naval operations in place of a payday?"

"I am aware of what I'm telling you. I'm also acutely aware that giving you this information puts an immediate target on my back. Not that I don't already have one. Everyone at this table does right now. How are you going to deal with that, Keith?"

"We are working on it. My plan is to put you all in a safe house for now. One that has been decommissioned so there are three people total that would even know that you are there. That way we keep the circle small with people that I would trust with my own life."

He looks around the room to get a sense of like or dislike for this plan. Everyone seems agreeable for now.

"I'm here for another reason as well. Emily, the police were unable to get much info from the deceased found at the scene. They did find these with him and I encouraged the officers to release them to me as they are not needed for any part of their investigation."

Keith puts an evidence bag with two rings into her hand. The wedding bands the kid went to pick up that morning. A painful reminder of the life she lost and the future she won't have with him. It truly is a cruel twisted fate that those symbols of love and longing are what's left after his life was abruptly severed from reality. She takes a trembling breath as her fingers curl around the bag before her shaking hand gives it back to him.

"Keep those until this is finished. I can't bring myself to look at what he had engraved on my ring until this is all over." Her breath catches in her throat, letting out an audible sad sound.

He nods and continues, "At this time, they can release him to you. Do you have a place that we can transfer him to for you?"

Her eyes fill with tears. I know we are sworn enemies after what I've put her and her family through, but part of me feels a little bad for her. Maybe it's because I'm worried about my own family. Another thing I never thought I would say in my life. Maria and Miggy awoke a small piece of me that occasionally feels something other than anger and hate. Thankfully it's only temporary or my role as the neighborhood bad guy would be much more difficult. Paul and Maverick embrace her in a hug as Keith waits for an answer.

"We can have them take Xander to the same place that we had mom, dad, and David's service. They offer many services, cremation is one of them, Emme."

Her blank stare tells me she truly loved that kid. She nods in agreement and Keith leaves the room to make the call.

"Keith?" she stops him before he leaves the room.

"Yes, Emily."

"I would like to have a service as soon as possible. Will you notify his parents for us? Have them get here as soon as physically possible before we get put into your safe home."

"I'm sorry but that won't be happening. You all have a very large target on each of you. I will not bring his parents into this. Once this is finished, you can have your service. You will be placed into protective custody with myself and two other agents before I leave this warehouse."

"No, we won't. You and your agents will wait until I put the love of my life to rest. This isn't up for discussion. Now make the call please."

"You are right, it isn't up for discussion. Now grab whatever items you need because my agents will be here soon to move you."

Keith leaves the room.

* * *

I need to get a message to Maria. But I'm sure her phone is being traced somehow. I'll see if Keith can get a message to her to have her leave for a few days. Find someplace to hide until this is over. Hopefully, the last package I sent her will help them start fresh somewhere new.

He walks back into the room. "The funeral home has

been called. One of my men will grab the ashes from there when they are available. These are burner phones; you will be disposing of your other phones before we leave this warehouse."

Keith drops several phones on the desk and starts to walk away again.

I look over toward Paul and try to get his attention.

"Paul, while we have a moment, I need to discuss something with you."

"What is it?"

We walk away from everyone else.

"If something were to happen to me, I need you to get a message to someone. On my desk at my home office, there's a photo. Behind the photo inside the frame is a name and number. I need you to call that number and let her know what happened and that I made sure she and my son will be taken care of."

That got his attention.

"You have a son, Ted?"

"Yes, in Ecuador. Maria is his mother and Miggy is my son."

"I see what you did there. You were always a huge fan of Miggy."

"My son enjoys playing baseball as well. It makes my cold black heart actually feel something when I watch him play. Anyway, will you do that for me, old friend?"

"Consider it done."

EMILY

Maverick comes into the office to check on me. "You about ready, Emme?"

"What are you going to do about Mel and Evelyn, Maverick?"

"I talked to Keith about that right before I came in here. He wants that plan to continue. If it goes past the five days, he will have me call her. They will pick her and Evelyn up and bring them to the safe house with us. He thinks they are safer right now being far from here. And us for that matter."

"I don't like that idea. I think they need to be with us, Mav."

"Normally, I would agree with you little sister but right now, we don't know if we are even going to be safe at this safe house."

He makes a valid point. "Okay, two more days and we make the call."

"I would call them right now if I thought it was safe for them."

* * *

Keith tells us his men are getting vehicles together and then they will be on their way. Maverick and I are still talking so I ignore him for a moment.

"Not to interrupt but the funeral home did call back and confirmed he's been transferred if you would like to make the call, Maverick, to give them Emily's wishes," Keith interjects.

Maverick leaves the room to make the arrangements for Xander.

"Emily, I will have someone pick him up as soon as possible. You have my word."

I have no words for him right now so I brush past him purposely hitting him with my shoulder on my way to the other room.

The tears start to pool in my eyes again when I go through the events of the past few days. It doesn't seem real at all. How did we get here? We were so happy and then in the blink of an eye, it was all gone. I don't have time for these feelings yet. I need to end this. Finish the mission. Trying to regain my composure I take a few deep breaths as Mav calls my name.

"Emme?"

I wipe my face to hide my tears even though Maverick knows how I feel.

"Yes, Mav?"

"The home can have him ready tomorrow. I already let Keith know."

"I appreciate that, thank you."

"Is there anything else I can do right now for you?"

"No but thank you."

"The Navy made an official announcement about Stanley. They suspect foul play and it's currently under investigation. Nobody has been named as a suspect at this time though. Maybe we have someone helping us after all."

"Queen takes over the board. That was the whole point right? She can control everything, even the narrative of murders she had people commit for her. I'm sure it's a matter of time before someone else is blamed for this. It sure won't be her though."

"Seems to be her whole plan. I wonder what she expects to gain from all of this?"

"Maverick, what does anyone want in a role like hers?"

He looks at me with a blank look on his face and then replies, "The title? That's what I would want after all my years of experience."

"The title yes but she mainly wants power. It's a political play for her. She wants more and more power. But I have every intention of shutting her down before she ever sees any of it."

Uncle Paul walks into the room and says that Keith and Abbott want to go through the plan for the safe house. We follow him into the main room and wait for one of them to talk. Keith starts.

"We will leave here shortly. My team, the one I mentioned earlier will be here with three floral delivery vans. We need to blend in, not stand out. We will then take you all to the safe house. From there, there will be no contact with the outside world, except for Maverick who will alert Mel that you all are safe and that my team is going to get her and bring her to him."

"When do we start working on our plan to get SECNAV?" I ask.

"The objective right now is to get you someplace safe and not known to anyone else. You all were witnesses to a major drug Cartel operation that has her involvement. My priority is keeping you safe now that your lives are in jeopardy."

"What happens if we don't go with you?

"Then we can't protect you, Emily."

My eyes dart around the room between him, Abbott, and my remaining family. A knot of fear and doubt twists in my stomach. My hands clench into fists, my eyes fill with tears.

"Is that what you told Xander, Keith. Leave me the fuck alone." I walk to the backdoor of the warehouse then turn to address the room, "I need to be alone for a bit."

ABBOTT

*K*eith asks, "Does anyone else need a moment here?"

"I think we get the point, Keith. Maybe give everyone some time to digest everything that's happened," I tell him.

His phone rings and he leaves the room. This time I wait only a moment before quietly following behind him. He heads to the room that Maverick originally had me in for questioning. I wait on the other side of the wall while I listen.

"What do you mean my name ended up on an OFAC (Office of Foreign Asset Control) list?"

There's a silence.

"I haven't sent any wire transfers or received any."

Another silence.

"Wait. How many times did my name come up?"

A brief pause

"And what names were used each time?"

I lean closer because I don't think he's hung up but he isn't saying anything.

"Have Dean look into this, please. I want a call tonight about the result."

I move into a small closet across the hall to avoid being seen.

After I feel that the coast is clear, I emerge from the small cleaning closet to rejoin everyone out in the main warehouse area. Emily is still outside.

Walking up to Keith I ask him, "Am I going to the safe house or prison tomorrow? Not that it matters, I'm dead either way."

"You have proven yourself to be helpful so for now you will join us at the safe house. Abbott, can I ask you something?"

"You are going to anyway so what is it?"

"Would you be willing to put your life on the line for someone else?"

"After all the shit things I've done, I would be fine giving up my life for someone that deserves to be here; like Maria and Miggy. They deserve a chance at a life that isn't tarnished by my past. Because I sure don't deserve it."

"That's what I needed to hear."

Keith walks away after telling me that his men had trouble getting three floral vans that matched but now that they have obtained them, it's just a matter of time before they get here.

The day turns to late evening and everyone is starting to get on each other's nerves. When you put a group of people together that don't necessarily like each other, what would you expect? We all agree to call it a night and in a few short hours, we head to the safe house.

EMILY

*A*fter I walk outside, I have a seat at an old picnic table that has been worn from the weather. Sun has already set hours earlier. It must be after midnight. I look at my watch to confirm that it's closer to 2:00 a.m. There's a gentle breeze in the air this morning. Thinking back to our conversation earlier with Keith. He told us that the FBI has run with a story that there was a gas leak in the building Xander was in. That's what they told the newspaper while they continue their search for Gabriel, the drug Cartel contact. It makes me wonder how many stories are just that. Stories that someone else made up to direct your attention away from it while they look into the real issue. "They" being whatever agency is involved.

Heading back inside I head straight to the office again to wait for the team that is on the way to take us to the safe house.

An hour and a half later, I hear vehicles pull up outside.

Maverick and Uncle Paul walk into the room.

"It's time, Emily," Uncle Paul tells me.

* * *

We all gather the few items we have with us and head outside. It's so dark and the lights in the lot are burned out, how convenient. Keith tells Abbott to get into the first floral delivery van, Uncle Paul, Maverick, and I into the second one. The third is added security. After taking our assigned seats, we set off toward the safe house. Our driver tells us that it's a bit of a drive and if we are tired, we would have plenty of time to sleep. I take that as my queue to get as comfortable as possible in my window seat and try to sleep. It's too loud in the vehicle making it difficult to fall asleep. I reach for my air pods, open Spotify on my phone and select mine and Xander's playlist. Hoping the songs will lull me to sleep. The first song that comes on was going to be our first dance song "Only Wanna Be With You" as I lay against the window, I try to suppress all of the emotions rising to the surface.

The song ends and a few moments later the same song repeats. I check my app to see if I have it set to repeat, but I don't. I skip to the next song, it's the same song. I review the list of songs from our list and the same song is on here fifteen times. I would have never saved it that many times. *What is going on?* I think to myself. I pick a different song from the list and at some point, I must have drifted off to sleep.

I'm nudged awake by someone. "Emme, it's time to wake up, we're here," Maverick tells me.

Looking around, I see a wood cabin nestled deep within the woods. Getting out of the van, I see nothing else. I can't even find a road that we would have come in from. The trees are so dense almost as if they are providing a wall of protection for this cabin.

The walls of the safe house have vines and moss clinging to its exterior walls. It appears to be forming a natural fortress around the cabin. The front porch has a couple of rocking chairs that seem to be frozen in time. I'm sure they are for the security detail.

We all walk to the back of the vehicle to claim our few items and head inside. The vehicle that Abbott and Keith left in isn't here nor is the other one that was supposed to be tailing us. Thinking to myself, *I wonder if he took him in to lock him up.*

Maverick steps ahead of me and stops me before climbing the stairs into the cabin.

"Emme, I can't image what you are going through but I am here if you want to talk."

"I know, Mav, and I love you for that but I need time. Time to heal and then plan what the next step is. She can't get away with this. She needs to pay."

"She will, Emme. If it's the last thing I do, I will help you get retribution for all of our loved ones."

"Thank you, Mav. I'm gonna head inside and lie down for a bit."

He moves out my way and lets me pass him.

Once we step inside, the interior reveals a cozy, rustic charm. Sunlight filters through the window near the door. Furnishings are simple in the main area. The security detail directs me to a room toward the back of the cabin. "Ma'am, this will be your room. Let me know if you need anything and I will see what I can do."

I thank him and close the door.

A few moments later there's a knock at my door. "Yes?"

"It's me, Emme, I brought you a couple of sandwiches. I don't know when you ate last but I know you need to eat something."

Opening the door, I see Maverick standing there with

two plates and some bottled water tucked under his arm. I move to let him in.

"Keith and Abbott here yet?" I ask him.

"Not yet. I'm not sure what's going on with that."

"I wonder if Keith thought Abbott would be a flight risk being out here away from civilization and decided to take him in now."

"That might be it."

"Maverick, you don't have to babysit me. Give me time."

"I'm not babysitting you; I came in here to make sure you ate something and to start discussing our plan to take down SECNAV."

"That we can do. Where do we start?"

Maverick and I must have lost track of time as the sun outside is starting to shift directions for the day. It was barely rising when we got to the cabin. There's another knock at my bedroom door.

"Yes?"

"Emily, I have something for you."

I look to Maverick who shrugs his shoulders as I move to open the door. One of Keith's men is standing there with an urn in his hands. Reaching for it, I nod my head, quietly thank him, and close the door.

"Do you want to be alone for a bit, Emme? We can finish this discussion later."

"Yes, thanks, Mav."

He hugs me briefly and then exits the room closing the door behind him. I set the urn on my end table and stare at it. It's hard to believe that an entire human can fit into this one container. Every bit of their existence scooped into this jar. All your precious belongings that some feel are so important to have, are now abandoned to collect dust. Dust is what you become when your life is taken from you and you are cremated. My mind continues on down this spiraling rabbit hole.

"Xander, you have always been my person. The one that I ran to when I needed to talk or vent about my brothers being assholes. The person who knew all my secrets. You could make me laugh by simply looking at me with one of your silly looks. Everyone should be so lucky to find a person like you. I will love you always and will forever be your girl. I'm sorry you weren't able to tell us about your assignment. I'm not mad at you anymore for it. I still don't understand, but the anger is gone. Well, the anger toward you. I am vehemently pissed at Keith still. That one is going to take a bit longer to get over."

"Our wedding would have been a little over a week from now. I think about how we were supposed to grow old together." Staring out the window, I try to force the tears to not fall. They aren't listening though as they free fall down my cheeks. Pressing my fingers to my lips, I then press them to the urn before leaving the room to see where we go from here.

ABBOTT

Keith drives for a while before taking our van we are in off to a different direction.

"We aren't going to the safe house, are we?"

"No, I need your help with something. We have a lead on Gabriel. Do you want to finish this, Abbott?" Keith asks me.

"What do you need from me?"

"We are heading to a location from which we believe he's doing business. I'm sending additional support to the location as well for backup. After what happened at the restaurant, we aren't taking any chances. Once we get there, you need to go in and distract Gabriel.

"He's liable to kill me as soon as I walk through the door."

"I have to hope that he wants an explanation from you and allows you to talk for a bit. Tell him you've been looking for him and turn the tables on him. Blame him for the warehouse situation."

"Can I ask why are you wanting me to poke the very

unstable bear? Not that I give a shit but some insight might help me determine the approach I take."

"We received some intel that he might be planning another attack and soon. If he's working with SECNAV he has your names all on a short list. We are trying to get ahead of that."

"By having me confront him head-on?"

"Yes."

"He doesn't trust me now. He accused me of setting him up at the warehouse."

"We know that. I'm not asking you to gain his trust. I'm asking you to distract him. We need to get in there and restrain him. If we go in like we did last time with the smoke bombs, he's liable to evade us again and this time we might not be so lucky."

"Lucky?"

"That he stayed here rather than going back to Ecuador. He has unfinished business here and he's trying to see that through."

"He's going to have me immediately checked for a wire. I won't go in wearing one."

"Understood. We will place the tiniest camera and microphone on your shirt. From a distance, it will look like the brand emblem of your shirt."

"It doesn't matter what you do or send me in with, this is a suicide mission and I know that."

Keith doesn't respond to my last comment. While I know how this will end, I can't help but think about my family. I will never see them again after tonight. And I've made my peace with that. Guys like me that have done the things I've done, don't deserve a life that is restful. But Emily has her whole life ahead of her. At one point, Mike and I were good friends, but then greed got in my way. I can't make up for my past or what I took from her, but I can give her a better future if I help end this.

"You can say no, Abbott, this wasn't part of the agreement."

"No, I need to do this in order to end this. I want to take this guy down. You know there are others like him, right? He isn't the main contact I usually meet with. He's the one that came this time but there will be others."

"We also know that. Gabriel is a start. A way to send a message to the Cartel letting them know we are on to them."

"You are willing to wake that beast?"

"If it means shutting down the operation sooner rather than later? Yes, we are willing to do what it takes. Are you?"

"I'm still in this car, aren't I?"

I think about the moments that I've taken away from Emily by killing Mike and then having Asher kill David. I let that sit with me for a moment. Miggy didn't have me as a pivotal person in his young life. I'm sure he will forget about me over time. Emily though will always remember what I took from her. She will never forgive me for taking away moments that she never got to have with them and I'm okay with that. I never expected to be forgiven, sometimes a person can only move on.

"Keith, do you have a pen and a piece of paper? Doesn't have to be big. I need to write something down for you to give to Emily. If things go as I feel they might, I would like you to give it to her please."

"In the glovebox, there should be a notepad and pen. Help yourself."

I grab my requested items and jot down what I want to tell her. After folding it up, I place the note and other items back in the glovebox.

* * *

We drive for a bit longer in silence. Keith doesn't ask me anything else. He seems satisfied with my answers and willingness to help.

After several more minutes and several deliberate turns, we end up on a street that has a few older buildings that appear to be in the renovation stage. Behind those buildings is an old-looking building designed to look like a barn. A large "For Lease" sign is posted on the lot. Keith pulls behind the barn building and parks.

He turns to give me directions to my intended target.

"One block up is a building that resembles a singlewide trailer. In that trailer is Gabriel and we believe two other people. There are technically two ways into that trailer. The front door and a sliding back door but the sliding door has something in front of it. A piece of furniture it would appear. It's blocking the majority of the view into the building. I'm sure it was deliberate. You will go through the front door, don't knock. Walk in, display your hands to show you are unarmed and try to immediately get his attention."

"In the short time I dealt with this Gabriel, he doesn't seem to be one for small talk."

"We will be right outside once you walk in. He doesn't have anyone watching the building. Once we located him, we have had people monitoring his activity and the same few people are seen coming and going."

"Here's to hoping I make it past the threshold."

"We will see you on the other side, Abbott. Thanks for working with us on this."

"I don't feel like I had much of a choice but if I'm going to go down, I'm fine with taking Gabriel with me."

I exit the vehicle and walk around the barn and over a

block to the trailer Keith told me about. It looks like a simple house from the street. You wouldn't guess that there is a psychopath that works with a drug Cartel inside.

Walking up the wooden stairs to the front door, I try the knob and it turns. Moving quickly I enter the trailer.

Within a split second I have two guns pointed in my direction.

"Abbott, I thought you were dead," states Gabriel.

"I'm sure you are disappointed by the fact that I'm not. It was a solid attempt though."

"You set me up, what reaction did you expect from me?"

"Funny, I was going to tell you the same thing. I figured that was all part of your plan, get your accounts setup and blow everything and everyone up in your wake."

"It does sound like something I might do, but I can't take all the credit for it. My men planned the bomb. I simply gave them the order to follow it through. Why are you here, Abbott?"

"To finish this. I told you I had a place for you to clean your money. But you blew that to literal bits. There's a backup place. A laundromat near the base. Tons of business. I bet with the right offer, we can get it. It's ready to go, no renovations or anything. You can start funneling money now if you wanted to."

"You could have walked away, I thought you were dead. What's in this for you?"

"You know the people I work for, there isn't a way out of this. I'm who they sent to see this through."

Something catches the corner of my eye. There's a room off toward the sliding back door. There's a light on and I can hear talking. I can't make out the voices though. Directing my attention back to Gabriel, I ask him if we can consider the new location I mentioned.

"This might work. This trailer won't last long before we are discovered. We were planning to move tomorrow to a different location. Set up a call with the realtor for the new place, I will pay thirty percent over asking."

The front door bursts open and several men come into the room, guns at the ready. I hear Keith give an order for Gabriel and his men to put their weapons down.

Gabriel and his men start to fire. I can see Gabriel looking around trying to find a way out but like Keith said, the back door is blocked by a very large piece of furniture. I assume it was so people couldn't see in. It makes it similar to shooting fish in a barrel with the DEA and Gabriel's men firing at each other and only one way out.

I move to the room by the back door. One of Gabriel's men already came out of there but I heard two voices earlier. Bullets are whizzing through the air with deadly intent. The sound is deafening in this small space. My heart is pounding as I reach the door. Reaching for the knob, I'm shot from behind. Any normal person's gut feeling would tell them to run, save themselves.

Feeling the burn as the bullet rips into my shoulder, it doesn't feel like a significant hit, but it does burn like hell. Throwing myself into the room, I start to look around. My eyes focus on something. Dropping my head down, I know what I need to do. I open the door, keep my hands in the air so they know I'm unarmed. The main area of the trailer has become a battleground. It doesn't matter though. One of Gabriel's men is injured near where I stand. I lean down to pull his weapon out of his hands. Keeping low to the ground I shift my eyes quickly looking for Gabriel. He's nowhere to be found again. One of Keith's men tries to get to me but before he makes it, shots are fired in my direction. I grab Gabriel's downed man and use him as a shield to deflect the bullets. The damage to my shoulder is more than I realize though making it difficult to pull him to me quickly. Another bullet hits me. This time in the chest. Falling to my knees, I can feel the blood filling up my lungs. I begin to choke on my own blood as I collapse all the way to the ground. Gunfire is still around me. I try to use the little amount of strength I have left to place my body in front of the room to create a barrier. My body starts to feel cold; the hail of gunfire starts to cease. I close my eyes. I feel nothing now.

EMILY

After allowing myself a chance to cry in private to say my goodbyes to Xander's ashes, I decide to check on Uncle Paul and Mav. Walking into the main room of the cabin I see Uncle Paul, Mav, and two security guards.

"Where's Keith and Abbott?"

"They had something to do before heading here," says one of the guards.

"What do you mean? What are they doing?"

"Everything will be explained soon enough."

God, I fucking hate when people are so vague! I think to myself. Taking a seat in the living room area I notice that there isn't a television or really much of anything that would require too much electricity.

"How long do you think we will be here?" I ask one of the guards.

"That's not for me to know, Ma'am. I'm sure Keith will provide more insight once they arrive."

I take in the room and notice there are zero windows in this bigger space. A few pieces of furniture and over on a coffee table are some very dated magazines. Past that is a small bookcase of old, worn books and a few decks of cards. The walls have nature-inspired artwork.

One of the guards offers to make us some dinner in the small kitchen. While modest in its size, has modern appliances, ready to provide sustenance for us, but no room for more than one person to be in at a time. The guards tell us that the walls are reinforced and there's a hidden door in the floor that leads to an escape route if needed. It's essentially an impenetrable fortress against any potential threats.

In the middle of the wilderness, this secluded cabin is more than a dwelling; it is a sanctuary of safety and solace, offering refuge to those in need. Today we are the ones in need of safety and shelter.

Once dinner is done, we sit around a small wooden table in silence and eat our food. As we are cleaning up our plates, we all hear a car pull up outside. Abbott and Keith are finally back. After cleaning my dishes, I head back to my room to settle in for the night. I figure whatever they did or were doing, we can talk about it tomorrow.

* * *

I pull back the covers on the bed and start to crawl in. There's a light knock on the door as I get my pillow adjusted just right. Letting out a heavy sigh after just getting comfortable, I climb out of the bed and open the door. My mouth falls open, my legs lose all feeling.

EMILY

"Hey, Ems."

I wake up cradled in Xander's arms. After I start to breathe again, I snuggle closer to him. "Xander, what the hell happened? You were gone? Your ashes are on that pathetic excuse for an end table over there."

"I have so much to tell you but first let me look at you."

He holds my face in his hands and I can see that he has a black eye and bruising all over his face. I lightly trace the marks with the tips of my fingers. Pulling him gently down towards me to give kisses along the trail my fingers just were. "Does it hurt?"

"Not anymore."

Keith is standing behind us in the doorway.

"Xander, we still need to debrief you," Keith interjects.

"I'm going to need a moment here, buddy. You all took fucking long enough to find me, you can wait."

He pulls me to him and leans in to kiss me.

"Xander, do you have any idea how hard it's going to be to get my fucking name off the SDN list of OFAC because of you?"

"Phone a friend, Keith, I don't fucking care." He turns back to me and pulls me into a hug. I smell him. His woodsy smell still clings to him. It's really him. He's here holding me. How is this even possible?

The door is pulled closed as Keith gives us some time alone.

"Does anything else hurt you, Xander?"

"No, I'm fine."

He helps me to my feet. Once I'm sure I won't pass out again, I launch myself onto him wrapping my legs around his waist as he carries me to the small twin-size bed. He carefully lays me down and stares at me.

"I never thought I would see you again. The intense pain I had in my chest thinking about not seeing you again was a feeling that I never want to experience ever again."

He crushes his lips onto mine. We hastily remove our clothes and explore each other's bodies while giving into all the emotions that have been building the past few days. I can't stop the tears as they fall. Not because I'm sad but because I have never been happier or in love as I am right now. The feeling of his skin touching mine, his searing kisses across my chest, and the feel of him entering me are all feelings I thought I would never have again.

We spend the next hour exploring each other as if it were the first time. There's a peaceful silence in the room. Only the sound of our breathing is heard. He grabs my hand and pulls me on top of him. It's then that I notice his smile isn't reaching all the way to his eyes. Something's wrong. I rub my fingers trying to relieve the wrinkle of worry from his forehead. "What is it, Xander?"

"Ems, we need to talk. I know this is a terrible time to have this conversation but this is bigger than you know."

At the same time, we say, "SECNAV is behind all of it."

"You know?" he asks me.

"Yes. How did you find out?"

"Before the building blew up, I tried to run to the front of the old restaurant. One of Gabriel's men grabbed me. He was the size of Dwayne "The Rock" Johnson. It was so sudden. He flipped me over his shoulder with that movement I dropped our rings. Once he got me outside, he threw me into their car. There were smoke bombs going off so nobody saw us leave. They also grabbed that Pierce guy but shot him and threw him in the trunk. We drove for what felt like forever to some trailer in the middle of nowhere. Gabriel ordered me to make new offshore accounts and shell companies because the other account numbers were lost in the fire.

"Wait. So, that explains why the rings were with the body that was in the building?"

"I was holding onto them when I was making the original accounts. As a reminder as to why I was doing this. For us. Well, for you, to make it so you didn't spend the rest of your days in a prison cell. But yes when he grabbed me, I dropped them."

"Prison cell? What are you talking about?"

"Keith approached me with some information that he had about your dad. It was more about Abbott and this whole EM-Comm thing they have with the Cartel. He needed my help and showed me evidence of Asher. They found his body and when they checked it for DNA, they found yours all over him. They also had a witness that saw you both together at the bar."

"So, Keith told you that?" I throw my clothes on quickly and head out of the room to confront Keith.

Xander jumps up and grabs my wrist.

"Ems, wait. He showed me the proof and that's all I needed to agree to the deal. I will do whatever to keep you safe. Always."

Dropping my head to his chest, I let out a heavy sigh.

"Why didn't you tell us? We could have helped."

"I was highly encouraged not to. For your safety and everyone else's. I would have never forgiven myself if something happened to you or your family."

"Sorry, back to the rings and the body... or ashes that are sitting on my end table. So, who is in there?"

"When the smoke bombs started, one of Gabriel's men grabbed me so quickly they dropped from my hand. They must have landed near whoever was left there. I overheard that one of Gabriel's men got shot in the crossfire. I assume it was him."

"How did you get away?"

"Well, that's what Keith is pissed about. I tried to signal to you by adding our song to our playlist over and over again but I guess you didn't listen to it. And I get that, Ems, if I thought you were gone, I wouldn't be able to listen to it either. I had to resort to plan b which is why his panties are in a twist. He was added to the SDN list for OFAC."

"What is that?"

"It's a list to keep track of possible terrorists or terrorist organizations that are setting up accounts or wiring money."

"Why was he on that list?"

"Because I added his name. Four times."

"But how did you access that list, Xander? That's the Department of Treasury site, right?"

"Yes, but I had to get someone's attention. It was the quickest way. I used his name and made the address something unbelievable using the safe word he gave me from my mission. From there I kept sending the same signal out trying to give them my IP address to narrow down where I was. With that and the fake address, they found me after a couple of days. I was completely surprised to see Abbott show up, though."

I am completely still when he says Abbott's name. He never made it to the safe house.

"Wait, Abbott?"

"Yep. I heard him as he walked in and tried to play off the whole incident at the original location. The old restaurant. Gabriel wasn't buying it at all. Abbott kept trying to convince him and almost did until Keith's men came into the building guns at the ready. When Abbott tried to run, he was shot but only in the shoulder I think the first time. He came into the room they were keeping me in and tried to protect me. He gave himself up from what Keith tells me. He went down in a gunfire blaze of glory while still trying to keep people out of the room I was in. It felt like many minutes had passed before Keith announced himself and came into the room where I was. He had to have Abbott removed from the door before they could come in.

"Xander, you are a legit genius with the OFAC thing. I'm not sure anyone else would have thought of that in the same situation. As far as Abbott is concerned, I will always be grateful to him for giving you back to me, but I can't forgive the past."

"Honestly, Ems, I don't think he would ever expect you to forgive him. I think he was trying to help you finish this. He didn't know I was in that room, but I saw the look on his face when he realized I was. It was a look of determination. Like he knew what needed to be done and he was the only one that could handle that responsibility. He gave me back my life and the chance to be with you. I will forever be thankful to him for that."

I jump back into his arms and squeeze him so tight while planting kisses all over his face all while trying to not hurt him."

A part of me feels bad for Abbott but the other part is incredibly thankful that he gave me Xander back. After all the pain and hurt he's caused through the years, maybe it was his way of redeeming himself.

Xander steps back briefly to look down at me.

"I do need to go talk to Keith but when I'm done, we are getting married. I don't care if it's in the kitchen and Mav gets ordained from the internet. It's happening tonight. My biggest regret was not marrying you before this all started. My second was not telling you the truth and I vow to never keep anything from you ever again."

I can't help but cry. This feels too good to be true. I must be dreaming and I know I'm going to wake up at any moment. He can't really be here right? If I am dreaming, I don't ever want to wake up.

"Xander, it's good to see you, son," Uncle Paul tells him as he slaps him on the back.

"Great to be seen, Sir."

"Xander, it's time, kid. We need to debrief and then you can go back to catching up."

Before they disappear into another room I call after him.

"Hey Keith? Why didn't you tell me he was alive this whole time?"

"Because I wasn't sure it was him, Emily. I didn't want to give you any false hope. I saw the anger in your eyes when you met me for the first time. You thought I took him from you forever and I don't blame you at all for the vitriol that you had for me. But I knew that if I gave you any small glimmer of hope and then was wrong, you would make sure I died a very slow painful death. I've pissed off many women in my day, but none of them made me nervous like you, Emily."

Xander lets out a belly laugh and it is the most beautiful sound I've ever heard.

"I have something for you. Abbott wanted to make sure you got it if something happened to him."

I take the folded piece of paper and for now tuck it into my pocket.

Xander turns back to me and grabs my hands.

"Ems?"

"Yes?"

"When I get back in here, will you marry me? I wasn't kidding. I'm done waiting."

"Yes, Xander, I will marry you the minute you get back in here."

He holds me for a moment longer, kisses my forehead, and follows Keith to a back room in the cabin.

"Mav, you need to get ordained."

"What? How am I going to do that, we don't have internet service here, Emme."

"Well, we are getting married tonight."

Xander is gone for a few hours. Mav tries to keep me occupied by telling me that he called Mel. She and Evelyn are on their way to meet one of Keith's security guards. They should be here in a few hours. I'm thrilled that we will all be together but I'm starting to get restless. As soon as I get up to check on him, he and Keith emerge out of the room they were in.

"Your country thanks you for your cooperation and service, Xander. Sadly, nobody outside of this room will know about it."

"That's fine with me. I did it for my girl not for recognition. Now if you don't mind, I would like to marry her. Now."

"Xander, we can't get Maverick ordained, safe house and all, no internet."

"We are still doing this. We can make it official later as soon as we are out of here. Keith gave me back these. He said you couldn't look at them yet. Are you okay with using these still?"

He opens his hand and the rings that we had made are in his palm. His is engraved with *My Heart You Keep.* When he hands me mine, I can see that it's engraved with *Always my girl.* I look up at him and nod my head letting him know that we can use these rings. Now more than ever they signify the life we get to have together. We agree to wait a little longer so Mel and Evelyn can be here as well.

Two hours later there's a knock on the cabin door. The other two guards ask us to wait behind them while they check it out. When they open the door, I hear in the sweetest southern accent. "Can one of ya'll help me with this stuff please?"

Mel and Evelyn are standing in the doorway. Mel is holding three different bags. One of the guards is grabbing more items from the floral van. Maverick runs over to hug his wife and daughter. They go off into another room to catch up. We give them some time.

Once they emerge from their room, Mel hugs Xander and I and tells us to make it official.

Xander and I exchange rings, no vows right now. Just a promise to love and protect each other. I kiss him like it's the first time. His lips are tender and soft. They convey affection, warmth, and our deep emotional connection. Slow at first and then I get lost in all my emotions rushing in again. We break apart when we feel tears on our lips. We are both crying because we never thought we would get this moment. This moment will be unforgettable. This image will imprint itself on my memory leaving a mark that I will always carry with me. It feels like I'm coming home.

***

A few weeks later, we are all completely cramped in this safe house. We have heard rumblings that Gabriel has gone back to Ecuador. Somehow, he managed to evade being captured when they rescued Xander. Something about jumping out of a window.

His one remaining guard was happy to give up his address but once the DEA got there, he was gone and the place was completely empty.

Uncle Paul snuck away from the safe house one night but not before telling us that he had something he needed to do for an old friend. He couldn't tell us when he would be back but that he would in fact be back.

Because of that, Keith is looking for another safe house to move us to. The way Keith explained it to us is that if my uncle were to be taken and tortured, he wouldn't be able to tell them where we were. I get it but I'm a little sad that if he were to come back here, we would be gone. He is a resourceful man though so maybe all is not lost on him finding us.

The sun has been up for a few hours now and all I want to do is lay in this bed with Xander. Knowing we are going to have to move around a bit to continue to evade SECNAV and her minions weights heavy on my mind. We can't go back to the home we all have known for so long. There's this profound mix of loss, fear, heartache, and dislocation. When you leave behind something so familiar, it's like saying goodbye to a part of your identity.

At the end of the day, it was shelter, a place to relax or meet up with family. A place to go when we needed a break from reality or a recent deployment. I'm not sure I'll ever get to go back to the only house I've known. But that's all it was. A house.

I reach for the folded piece of paper that I haven't been able to bring myself to read yet.

Emily, live a life worth living; something I could never do. I stole your past from you, but I hope to allow you a future. As Mike would say, "Family above all."

Xander moves a little while I'm lost in my own thoughts about what I read. He's still asleep and looks so peaceful. Watching him sleep is probably my favorite thing right now because it means he's still here with me. He's my heart and my life. Where he is, that's where I will always want to be. He's my future. He's my home.

EPILOGUE

SECNAV Jack Cohen

In the grand, mahogany-clad office of the Secretary of the Navy, Jaqueline "Jack" Cohen, the air hangs heavy with tension. A report was delivered that leaves her seething with frustration and disappointment. The polished surface of her desk gleams in the dim light as she clenches her fists, her expression stern and unyielding.

You have high expectations for your team, for the navy, and for me. One would think that competence and dedication were non-negotiable. I demand excellence in every aspect of my work. But now as I stare at this report, it's clear that those I had entrusted with important responsibilities let me down.

I can feel my lips press into a thin line as I read through the details. My eyes narrow with each passing sentence.

The report outlines a series of blunders, oversights, and poor decisions made by Robert Stanley.

"I have hired a group of incompetent imbeciles. Where are the Fallons?"

"Ma'am, that's what I'm trying to tell you. We lost them. We know they are working with the DEA now. We think they have them at a safe house."

Frustration and anger course through me as I'm told about the Fallons slipping away again. My fingers drum impatiently on the surface of my desk, my frustration simmering beneath a calm exterior. I have no tolerance for mediocrity, especially when it comes to matters of national security.

"You find them now. I have every bit of confidence in the fact that you would choose to continue to live. For that to happen, you need to find them. Get with your team and review all the intelligence we have on whoever might be helping her. The hunt for them is far from over. Explore all your leads, leverage any contacts that you have, and find new tactics to bring them in."

"Yes ma'am. On it ma'am."

"You are dismissed."

Lieutenant Smith leaves my offices abruptly. I only brought him into the fold because of how closely he worked with Abbott for the past several years. I shall see how he handles his current orders to decide whether he stays on or becomes fish food in the Atlantic.

Leaning back in my leather chair, I click my pen while I think. A terrible annoying habit I've never been able to shake. Who can I trust now? Stanley is dead, Abbott is rumored to be dead as well, Pierce and Spencer are also no longer amongst the living. There's one chit I can call in. I've been holding onto it for awhile now with the hope that

I would never need to use it. I take a deep breath, pick up the phone and dial a familiar number.

The phone rings a few times before he answers.

"Why do I feel like I'm being called to the principal's office?"

"Agent Cortez, we have a situation. Call me back on a secure line."

My phone rings almost immediately after hanging it up.

"I need to call in that chit now. We've got a threat and we need to find Emily Fallon. She knows too much. I believe she's being held at a government safe house by the DEA. Find out who's holding her and let them know she's needed for questioning immediately."

There's a brief pause on the other end of the line before Agent Cortez responds.

"You called me Agent Cortez which makes this is a business call. Understood Secretary; you know I don't do this lightly. Are you sure about this?"

I clench my jaw as I weigh the gravity of my request. The implications of calling in such a favor is something I can't come back from. But the safety of the original mission hangs in the balance.

"I apologize for the formalities but yes this is a business call. I'm calling in that favor now. Emily is a person of interest in an ongoing investigation. We believe she is a threat to the American people and has crucial information that might help us to close a case. Her actions have left us with no choice. We can't afford to let her information fall into the wrong hands."

Agent Cortez sighs in a way that reflects his understanding of the seriousness of the situation.

"Okay, Jack, I'll pull some strings. We'll initiate the

operation and locate her. One question for you if I may, ma'am?"

"Yes, Agent Cortez?"

"Is this on the record for this particular operation?"

"This needs to be off the record."

"Copy that, Ma'am. We'll proceed with the operation discreetly. Are there any specific protocols or instructions you'd like us to follow?"

"I want this handled only by you and by any means necessary. You need to get the intel. From there, do what you need to do to keep her quiet. You will keep me and only me updated on your progress."

"Absolutely, Secretary."

With those words, a complex web of resources is set in motion. NCIS will work tirelessly to locate Emily and neutralize the threat she poses to the Navy. The stakes are high but I'm prepared to do whatever it takes to protect all of the secrets.

"Have her brought to NCIS to make it appear official. From there, use any means necessary to get the mission completed."

"Understood ma'am."

"And Agent Cortez"

"Yes ma'am?"

"If you need to quiet her, cover your tracks."

ACKNOWLEDGMENTS

First, I would like to thank my Husband. You challenge me in the best way possible. Without you, the books I write would not be nearly as fun. You are the only person that gets my truly twisted mind. You also helped to create the creepiest character I've written to date. Thank you for being my person. I love you more and I said it first.

To my children, thank you for taking an interest in my hobby. I know you will probably never read these books, but you ask about them and let me talk about them so thank you.

To my Alpha Readers, Eric and Jill, thank you for being straightforward with your comments and critique. You both make me a better writer.

My Beta Readers, Ashley, Chelsea, and Veronica from the bottom of my heart I thank you. Each of you took the time to provide feedback that was incredibly helpful. Thank you for being a part of my team.

To Shae, my cover designer, you are amazing! I had one request for the cover and you blew it out of the freaking park.

To my editor, Linda, working with you has been a dream. You are quick, concise, and have been such a valuable part of my team. Thank you for working with me on this project.

To my ARC team, I don't even know where to start except to say that I am truly grateful for each of you. I could not have done any of these without all of you.

Finally, to the readers, thank you for taking a chance on me. I hope you have loved following Emily's journey. We have one more book coming in 2024 to complete this trilogy.

ABOUT THE AUTHOR

Madeline Vaughn grew up in Kansas City, MO and is a graduate of the University of Missouri. Madeline and her husband live in Kansas City with their four boys. When they are not working, they spend their time traveling the country to find new locations to hike and inspiration for future novels. Follow her on Instagram-@madelinevaugnbooks or her website: www.madelinevaughnbooks.com

Printed in the USA
CPSIA information can be obtained
at www.ICGtesting.com
LVHW081030031123
762916LV00009B/129